STEALING AMY

A DARK ROMANCE

IZZY SWEET
SEAN MORIARTY

D1608076

Dirty Nothings

Copyright © 2017 by Izzy Sweet and Sean Moriarty

All rights reserved. This book or any portion thereof may not be reproduced or used in any manner whatsoever without the express written permission of the publisher except for the use of brief quotations in a book review.

Published by Izzy Sweet and Sean Moriarty

This is a work of fiction. Names, characters, businesses, places, events, and incidents are either the products of the author's imagination or used in a fictitious manner. Any resemblance to actual persons, living or dead, or actual events is purely coincidental.

Copyright © 2017 Izzy Sweet & Sean Moriarty

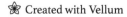 Created with Vellum

CONTENTS

ABOUT THIS BOOK

They grabbed the wrong girl.

They thought I was his wife, not the woman he's obsessed with.

Ivan Romanov is one of the Russian mafia's biggest financial backers.

And he's been destroying my life piece by piece just to get me in his bed.

I never wanted to be in this situation.

Stalked.
Cornered.
Desperate.

I was doomed. About to be forced by a powerful man who was willing to take what I didn't want to give.

Then he came, a demon in the dark. A dark voice that told me to be a good girl if I want to live...

NEWSLETTER

Sign up for our newsletter - no spam- and download an Izzy Sweet book for **free**

http://bookhip.com/CKHPSJ

1

ANDREW

T *hump.*

"I simply don't understand it, Bart. You had everything in the palm of your hand..."

Thump.

My fist connects again with his body and this time it elicits a muffled screech. That tends to happen when someone's kidneys have been hit hard enough. It's strange, for such vital organs, the body sure didn't keep them hidden inside somewhere safe.

The screams and screeches peter out until I slam my fist against the other kidney. If I was a gambling man, which I'm not, I would say that Bart would be pissing blood for a week if he wasn't destined to die pretty soon.

"You were a part of the inner circle. You had your mouth on the golden teat! How the fuck could you betray Lucifer?" I ask.

Standing in front of Bart, I shake my head at him. His

eyes are wide with terror, and if I'm not mistaken, he pissed himself recently.

"All you had to do was tell Lucifer the Japs had approached you. You could have told him they were trying to pay you off. You know for a fact he would have fixed you up. He always takes care of us!"

I don't mean to scream that at the end, but Bart has to have known that.

Loyalties have been tested in the past with some of the guys, and every time Lucifer was there to make sure we followed him. To make sure we knew he was as loyal to us as we are to him.

The shrill sound of my phone ringing from my suit pocket stops me from swinging at his eyes. My fist is inches away from his nose when I stop myself.

I grin at him.

Wagging a finger in his eyes, I say, "Not just yet, be right back. You just hang out for me."

I pull the phone out of the suit jacket I left hanging on the back of the shitty chair in this room. Everything in this shitty room is fucking way past its prime. Then again, if it wasn't an abandoned old motel out in the middle of nowhere it wouldn't be so shitty.

"This is Andrew."

"Andrew, my friend!"

"Harrold, I was going to call you soon... How're things going?"

"Busy, as you well know. Mr. Lucifer informed me you

would be needing my services today. I wanted to see if you had a time frame..."

Winking at a terrified Bart, I say, "Can you meet me at the old motel in about an hour? I won't be here much longer."

"I will be there."

"Thanks."

Disconnecting the phone, I put it back in my pocket before I pull the forty-five pistol from my shoulder holster. Bart is shaking now, and that wet spot I saw earlier is growing larger by the second.

The distinct smell of shit erupts in the air as I walk up to Bart and push the barrel of the pistol against his stomach.

"It's a shitty thing to know exactly how much more time you have left to live. To know you can't change the certainty of your own death."

Lowering the pistol towards his crotch, I pull the trigger.

The loud eruption of the gun in this small but tattered room deafens me. It's a few moments before I'm able to hear his loud screams through the ball gag I have crammed in his mouth.

"You're going to the afterlife a cockless bastard!" I roar over his screaming.

Aiming at his knee caps, I pull the trigger twice in rapid succession.

One in each knee cap.

The screaming continues for a few seconds before he

passes out, his head slumping forward. Pain has a way of breaking everyone. He's no different than any other pile of shit out there.

Not any more he isn't.

Fucking little bitch is now one of the commoners. One of the fucking sheep out in the fucking herd that gets to die when the big bad fucking wolves tear his throat out.

There's a code in this world, it's an oath to each other that binds us. It's there to make sure we have each other's back, no matter what.

What he did... It's just not done.

We are all hard, battle-tested men who want the most from our role in life. He just threatened that role. He removed himself from being above the common crowd and put himself down in the mud like the rest of the fucking pigs.

Rolling in filth and shit.

Sitting in the chair that my coat hangs on is the small black leather bag I brought into this shitty motel with me. It's a fucking dump here, and I pray that I don't get bugs from the shitty room.

Pulling a hypodermic needle out of the bag, I take the bottle of adrenaline out as well. I fill the syringe as I walk over to Bart.

Back when I was in the SEALs, I served as a medic. Normally, I would never pull someone from a blackout like this.... it fucks with the body and will probably hurt his heart and brain pretty bad.

But he doesn't need to worry about those things.

I inject directly into the heart. His head snaps forward in wide-eyed misery as he comes back to reality.

Walking back to the bag, I pull out a small bottle of morphine.

His hands are stretched high above his head and he hangs from the ceiling supports. It doesn't help with injecting the pain meds.

Shrugging my shoulders, I push the medicine into a vein throbbing on the left side of his neck.

The drugs must work pretty damn well because his eyes lose that pain-filled haze and slowly begin to focus on me. I didn't give him much though, just enough to dull the pain but not cloud the mind.

"Bart, I know you were one of us so I won't send you to be fed to the pigs while you are alive. You get that much out of me. But Lucifer has a reputation to protect and so do I. I'm going to use you as a message to the Japs. You won't be alive to give it to them, but I'm pretty sure they will understand it all the same."

Pulling a scalpel from the bag, I first slice off his right ear then his left.

The screams are audible through the gag again and I'm tempted to do this after he dies, but I don't think that would be the right thing. He betrayed Lucifer and put the wife and kids in jeopardy—that can't be allowed *ever*.

But more importantly, he betrayed me and the men who serve our boss.

Taking out my anger again, I punch him in the

mouth. I wince. Fuck, I think I hurt a knuckle with his teeth.

Shit, it's time to finish this off. I need a cold beer and a very hot pussy after shit like this.

He passes out sometime after I stab his eyes out.

No sight, no hearing, and no talking. He will go to them as a good message of what is to come for daring to attack us. To dare attack our boss.

Slicing the rope that is holding him up, his body falls to the ground in an almost boneless fashion. He's in the land of twilight now, not dead but almost.

I've never removed a tongue before and it makes my stomach quiver a bit.

My phone rings as I am unzipping my pants, my thick flaccid cock coming out of my boxers. "Fuck"

Walking over to my coat, I pull the phone out and walk back to the still-breathing body. I push connect at the exact moment I release a torrent of piss down on the bastard's face.

"Yeah?"

"We're here, Andrew."

"Ah, okay. Come on back, I'm done here."

My bladder comes to a stop as I finally empty it completely. Bart's face turns towards me and he makes a loud, pitiful groan.

Kneeling down beside him, I say, "I hope you find even more torment in hell."

Putting the pistol to his forehead, I pull the trigger, and again the roar of the gun is deafening to my ears.

2

AMY

One year later

I van's baby blue eyes flick towards me, full of apology, as he focuses most of his attention on the phone pressed against his ear.

My eyes meet his and I keep expecting to feel *something*. To feel something more than this coldness that seeps inside of me.

Whoever he's listening to must say something to make him angry because his eyes narrow, no longer focusing on me, and he speaks sharply in Russian.

Honestly, I don't care that he has a phone call. Anything that pulls his attention away from me is a welcome relief.

I just want this stupid date to be over with.

Glancing down at my salad, I stab a piece of romaine

lettuce a little more forcibly than required and push it into my mouth, chewing thoughtfully.

Ivan continues to speak rapidly in Russian and I don't understand a word he's saying except for the name *Lucifer*.

I never considered Ivan the religious type. In fact, I'm pretty sure the guy is a ruthless, heartless criminal who would sell his own mother if given half a chance. But more and more often lately, I keep hearing that name.

Has Ivan suddenly taken up faith?

It doesn't seem likely. Something else must be going on... Something that is pissing Ivan off.

Dropping my fork, I push my plate away and pick up my glass of wine. Slowly, my eyes glide over the room, taking in the upscale restaurant he brought me to. The décor is exquisite. Everything is done in white, gold, and sparkling crystal.

The clientele is impeccable; we're surrounded by the crème de la crème of Garden City. I recognize the mayor, a few A-list actors, and a rising pop star.

Everyone is dressed like they're ready to hit the red carpet or something—including the man sitting across from me.

Ivan looks like he just stepped off the cover of a magazine in his dark charcoal gray suit and blue silk tie. His suit jacket is unbuttoned, and he leans back in his chair. He is easily the most attractive man in the room, and it's done effortlessly.

He's beautiful, one of the most beautiful men I've ever

laid eyes on with his short, white blonde hair, and baby blue eyes. His bone structure is flawless. Sharp cheekbones, a straight nose, and soft, kissable lips.

But his beauty does nothing but leave me feeling empty. No matter how hard I try to connect with him the connection just isn't there.

Sipping my wine, I know I should be flattered that a man like him is interested in a girl like me. And in the beginning, I was flattered... but no longer.

I've glimpsed the monster behind the beautiful mask and now I can't unsee it.

Two shadows move behind Ivan and I drink deeper.

I'm totally fucked and I don't know how to get myself out of this mess. Those two shadows are guarding Ivan's back, and I know there are at least two more at each exit. I could try to slip away, but even if I do succeed, what about Abigail?

My heart starts to race and I quickly have to shut down my panic. Freaking out will only make this worse.

So what if I don't have an excuse tonight to keep him out of my bed? Maybe it won't even come to that...

Ivan's rapid Russian slows and his blue eyes focus once more on me. He watches me drain the remaining wine in my glass and makes a motion with his hand. A waiter lingering beside the table rushes forward, refilling my glass before I even get it back down to the table.

Ivan's soft lips spread into a pleased smile and he picks up his glass of vodka, cheering me before tipping it back.

His eyes never leave my face as he drinks, and I know he expects me to join him. I also know that if I refuse the invitation that it will most likely make him angry... so I pick up my glass and tip it back.

Ivan drains his glass and the waiter steps forward to refill it but Ivan waves him away. I finish off half of my glass, feeling the warm buzz of alcohol warming my belly before I set it down on the table gently.

Ivan motions for the waiter to refill my glass for me.

Clenching my teeth together, I watch the waiter top my glass off and my cheeks burn with heat.

So it's come to this? He's resorting to getting me drunk so he can finally sleep with me...

Lifting my glass, I drain down the wine, drinking deeply. I need the alcohol's false courage to fortify me so I can make it through this night.

Ivan smirks and his eyes warm as he watches me.

He's been trying to sleep with me for weeks now, and I'm not sure how I'm going to blow him off tonight. I'm running out of excuses.

How did my life come to this? Dreading the affections of such a man...

I bet half the women in this room would probably give their left tit to sleep with him.

They can have them if they want him.

I fucking hate him.

Eight weeks ago, Ivan walked into my life, and I wish he would have walked right back out of it. He walked into my work, a little clothing boutique downtown, looking for a present for his sister. Shamelessly, he flirted with me the entire time I helped him pick out a scarf. And given that he's so damn handsome, I was immediately taken with him.

I was over the moon when he returned the next week, and the week after that.

When he asked me out on a date, it was like a dream come true.

He's rich, beautiful, and powerful. And for those first couple of weeks, I wondered if I had somehow stepped into a fairy tale. He lavished me with expensive gifts and took me out to expensive restaurants. He even gifted me an entire new designer wardrobe.

But after a while, it was becoming very apparent that he expected me to repay him for the favors.

That was when the illusion started to fade for me. I began to notice his perfection was flawed. All the little things became more apparent. Still, I tried to return his affection, up to a point, but he always wanted more.

He demanded it.

I tried to break things off. I even attempted to return everything he ever gifted me, but he's a man who refuses to accept the word *no*.

After the first night I refused him, I started to notice strange men following me to work. They'd linger outside the boutique during my shift, keeping tabs on me and everyone I interacted with.

At night, Ivan would show up at my door, questioning me about my day, and becoming more and more obsessive. I became afraid, and even looked into a restraining order, but all that did was piss him off and show me just how powerful he truly is...

Ivan speaks a few clipped words into his phone and then hangs up. Tucking the phone into his pocket, he leans forward and grabs my hand.

I resist the urge to pull my hand away. Something about his touch makes my skin crawl.

"My apologies, *myshka*," he purrs, fingers wrapping around me tightly. "But that was a very important call."

I nod my head and set my empty glass down on the table. Ivan nods towards the glass and the waiter steps forward, refilling it once more.

Ivan pulls my hand towards him and then lifts it to his mouth, lips tenderly brushing across my knuckles.

For a moment, I wonder what is wrong with me. Something inside of me must be broken. This beautiful man is bestowing his affections upon me but I find his touch repulsive. No matter how hard I try, I can't bring myself to enjoy it.

Neither his beauty nor his money can make up for all his horrible faults.

He's controlling, and aggressive when he gets angry. He hurt me the last time I refused to let him through my apartment door. He shoved me into the damn wall and pulled out a chunk of my hair in front of my daughter Abigail.

I'm trapped. The best I can do right now is try to make him happy so he doesn't kill me...

I try to pull my hand away from Ivan's mouth and his fingers tighten around me, squeezing painfully.

I endure the compression for as long as I can before a yelp slips past my lips.

Ivan's eyes flash and then he grins as if I've somehow pleased him. His grip relaxes and I let my hand drop to the table before trying to pull it back.

I watch him warily until I have my hand safely in my own lap.

Leaning back, he flicks his fingers at his empty glass and his vodka is refilled immediately.

"Amy..." he purrs huskily.

Rubbing my hand beneath the table cloth, I make my expression as neutral as possible. "Yes?"

"Finish your drink."

Inside, I'm fuming. Reaching out, I grab my drink and it takes every ounce of self-control I have to keep from tossing it in his smirking face. He lifts his own glass and sips from it while watching me.

I bring my glass to my mouth and my stomach twists as I sip. Already, the wine is sour on my tongue and the warm buzz has become an annoying after-effect.

Our eyes meet over the rims of our glasses. His bore into mine like icy daggers until I finish the wine off completely. The glass empty, I'm afraid to set it back down on the table, afraid he'll order the waiter to refill it.

I lean back, keeping the empty glass in my grip.

Smirk sharpening, Ivan snaps his fingers and a body peels away from the shadows, one of his beefy bodyguards coming forward. Murmured words are exchanged between the two before a long, black velvet box is produced.

My eyes fall upon the box and I'm filled with dread and trepidation. Another gift? Please no...

Setting his glass down on the table, Ivan rises and approaches me, the box in his hand.

Watching him approach, I shake my head. "Ivan... You shouldn't have..."

Seriously, he shouldn't have. Every gift he's ever given me he's used to force some kind of repayment out of me. In the beginning it was sweet, he would only ask for another date.

More recently though it's become a kiss while his hands try to fondle me...

He plucks the empty glass from my hand and sets it on the table. Immediately the waiter comes forward and refills it.

"Ah, but I must, my *myshka*. Tonight is a special night, and I want you to remember it always."

Bending over me, he snaps the box open in front of my eyes. I blink at all the diamonds, their dazzling sparkles almost blinding me.

"It's too much... I can't possibly accept it," I protest softly as he lifts the strands of diamonds from the box.

Ivan clicks his tongue against the roof of his mouth as he wraps the strands around my neck. "It's only a trinket."

"A trinket?" I repeat incredulously. The three strands

are completely covered in diamonds, and I know they must be worth thousands.

"Yes," he says, his breath tickling my ear. "Only a trinket. When you give me my heir then I will present you with proper jewels."

Heir? What the fuck? This is the first I'm hearing of this...

Ivan buries his face in my hair and breathes in deep.

I shudder, wanting to rip the diamonds off of my neck.

"Come," he says, pulling away and grabbing me by my sore hand.

"Where are we going?" I ask, trying not to panic as he pulls me to my feet.

His arm wraps around my waist, bringing me close. "It's time to retire for the evening."

I shake my head and glance around, searching for an escape.

My eyes fall upon the table. "But I didn't even get to finish my drink..."

Ivan tips his head back, chuckling. Reaching around me, he grabs my glass and hands it to me. "Here, you can finish on the way."

Pushing the glass into my hand, I have no choice but to accept it. He gives me a pointed look until I lift the glass to my lips and drink.

Fuck it. If I have to endure this, I might as well be drunk.

Neck arching back, I drain the wine completely as he

guides me. His fingers flex around my hip protectively and he leads me to the back of the restaurant, through the kitchen, and to a door that opens to the back alley.

He has some silly rule about never leaving through the front.

I set the empty glass on a counter before we pass through the back door, stepping into the night. Ivan's black limo is idling and the chauffeur holds the back door open for us.

Ivan pauses for a moment, looking towards the two bodyguards in the alley before dragging me forward. We take three steps and then Ivan tenses beside me.

Dropping my hand, he whirls around, and everything happens so fast I'm not sure what is happening.

Ivan crumbles to the ground and one of his bodyguards approaches me.

For a hysterical moment, I want to thank the bodyguard for knocking out Ivan but then the man grabs me. His hand slaps over my mouth and my lips are stuck together, I can't move them.

I gaze up at the bodyguard, my eyes wide and watering as I scream behind the tape in panic.

His face hardens and then the world goes black.

As the black silk hood settles over my head and two strong arms lift me up, I can't help but feel a little relieved...

How fucked up is that?

3

ANDREW

Bagged and gagged. That went almost too easy, but for now, I'm not going to complain. Shit, I even have a hot fucking chick in the back with our package, but it's going to be a shame if I have to consider her excess baggage.

Lucifer doesn't like baggage when it comes to jobs. He wants everything neat and orderly. And this is a whopper of excess baggage.

We were supposed to take only Ivan and the wife, not his bimbo.

Snagging his fuck-toy was a must though when he brought the girl out the back door with him. If he hadn't been such a gigantic douche nozzle, manhandling her out the door like he did, we could have snatched him and left her in the dust.

Shit. Things like this only lead to fucking complications. I don't want complications. Fuck, it should have been his stupid fucking wife. Not this... this... fucking sexy young girl.

Shaking my head, I frown at the two people sitting across from me in the black limousine.

Turning my head, I tell Peter, "Let's get to the warehouse, but add a few minutes to the trip. I need to figure out what to do about our little complication."

Peter nods his head and I turn back to watch my prisoners for a few more minutes. The girl is sitting there, stiff as a board. Her every muscle looks locked in strain as she turns her head towards every little sound.

I bet she's coming to grips with her dire situation. I bet she knows she is a loose strand, like a weed that needs to be plucked from the garden.

I fucking hate killing women, it turns my stomach when I do it, but... Fuck. Stupid fucking Ivan is dooming her.

Leaning forward, I growl out, "You stupid fuck, Ivan."

Lashing out with a fist, I snap it into the bag that's hiding that shit-fuck's face. I feel the protruding bulge of his nose before the sharp stab of pain lances through my hand.

The scream of pain from behind his gag is just a little louder than my growl of, "Fuck!"

Shaking my hand, I hear a chuckle coming from the front seat behind me. I've fucked my damn hand up again. This damn hand has been nagging me all year.

Peter says, "Shit, did you just fuck your hand up again, Andrew?"

Ignoring him, I reach forward and whip the bag off of Ivan's head.

He's got fucking spirit though, I'll give him that. Bloody nose, tears streaking down his cheeks. He still looks pissed off. And if looks could kill? I'd be castrated.

Shaking my hand, I rub the knuckle that is sending sharp stabs of pain through it. I fractured the damn thing when I was taking care of Bart, and I haven't really had a chance to let the thing heal up.

Too many people are getting swept up into the maelstrom that is Lucifer's rage. It's been a year of fire and brimstone.

Too bad Ivan's on the wrong side of the fence right now. I'm positive he's never been on the receiving end of the treatment he's getting right now. Well, fuck him and his bitch ass looks. Dude isn't going to be such a pretty boy now.

That fucking broken nose will make sure of that.

"You've become a problem, Ivan. Now, usually Lucifer would handle things like you exclusively... But that's not how things are happening now. The inner circle has been unleashed on fucks like you."

He yells a bunch of words through the tape but they are too gargled to understand.

Shrugging my shoulders at him, I say, "Can't understand a single fucking word you're saying right now. I'd remove that tape from your mouth, but then you would probably be squealing like your bimbo over there."

Looking at her fully for a moment, I can appreciate what the man sees in this girl.

Her legs look fucking amazing. She wasn't put into the car gently, so the eyeful of legs and just a hint of exposed crotch is a pretty fucking hot sight.

She looks a little too elegant for someone like Ivan, too... She doesn't look fake like Ivan's wife does. No, this girl has never had the touch of a surgeon's knife.

From what I saw of her in the restaurant... fuck. If she was mine, I'd never let her out of my bed.

He screams at me again through the tape, and I can tell Ivan really doesn't appreciate me looking at his chick.

Fuck him.

Turning to look at him, I just can't take all the noise he keeps spurting out like some fucking stuck pig.

Leaning forward again, I slam my fist into his stomach. The air expels from his nose explosively and he loses all focus on me.

Turning my head to Peter, I say, "Take us to the warehouse. We'll see what Lucifer wants to do. We need this pile of shit out of the car. He smells like sour vodka and piss."

Amy

I can't see. No matter how much I blink my eyes, there's no light. No hint of anything around me. Only darkness.

This damn bag on my head is stifling.

At first, when I was grabbed and tossed into whatever

vehicle we're in, I was on the verge of hyperventilating. Panicking about my situation. But I cut that shit out quick. All it got me was my own hot breath in my face and that totally sucked ass.

Complication. They haven't outright said it but I know that's me. Whatever they have planned, I'm not supposed to be a part of it.

Somewhere near me is a man, a man with a very deep, rumbling voice, who is holding my life in his hands.

If I could beg or plead, I would. I'd get down on my knees and promise anything. But all I can do is sit here on this seat and pray that they realize I'm no threat. I won't talk about anything that's happened.

They only want Ivan... and fuck, they can totally have him. Whatever they have planned for him he probably deserves it.

My lips are sealed.

I know it's useless trying to do anything about this.

You see, I've already learned my lesson when dealing with these kinds of men. They do the things they do and get it away with it because they're not afraid of the authorities. They are the authorities in Garden City. Meting out their own rules and justice.

They have the police and the judges and everyone else above them in their pockets.

I learned this the hard way when I tried to get a restraining order against Ivan. Not only was my petition dismissed, the judge actually lectured me about wasting his time and advised me to make up with Ivan. He threatened to turn the authorities on *me*.

Beside me Ivan gurgles and I strain my ears, trying to listen over him. The man who spoke earlier is quiet now. Too quiet.

If only I could speak. If only I could say something...

I can sense him though. I can feel his eyes boring into me. All the little hairs on my body stand on end, pointing towards him.

I'm terrified of him, yet something about that fear also excites me.

I feel so fucked up for feeling like this.

The vehicle slows and comes to a complete stop. The engine turns off.

Fuck, this is it.

One of the doors opens, and I feel a burst of cold air hitting my legs. Ivan grunts and I sense a struggle beside me.

"Fuck, he does stink," someone mutters unhappily. "Come on, you stupid fuck."

The air beside me moves and then there's a thump. A body hitting the pavement?

"Really? You're going to make me drag you?"

There's a series of grunts and the gritty sound of gravel grinding against something.

I'm so focused on what's going on outside that I completely forget about the danger inside.

Suddenly a warm hand comes down on my bare thigh and I gasp, stiffening.

Strong fingers wrap around my thigh, digging into my flesh. But the grip doesn't hurt... No, there's something about it that's strangely possessive.

The fingers relax, flexing, and then they drag upwards. "You're going to be a good girl, yes?" the deep voice asks.

For a heartbeat I'm so terrified I do nothing. Then quickly realizing my mistake, I start to rapidly nod my head.

I'll be a good girl. I'll be so good, I try to mentally project to him.

I'll do anything to make it home to Abigail.

His hand reaches the apex of my thigh and then there's a pressure. Oh god... Does he want me to spread for him?

"If you do everything you're told," he growls and pushes harder, forcing me to open my legs for him. "I just might be able to get you out of this."

Might?! He *might* be able to get me out of this?

Once again I start to pant, my own hot little breaths hitting the bag.

His fingers move and then I feel them brushing against my panties. I freeze.

"Would be such a shame..." he mutters and then his hand pulls away.

The tension breaks and my lungs pull in much needed air. Before I can think too much about what he just said, or did for that matter, my arm is grabbed and I'm pulled out of the vehicle.

Stumbling, I try to get my bearings.

The cool air hits me and I shiver, straightening. Fingers tighten around my arm, pulling me forward.

My heels dig into gravel and I'm grateful for the firm grip that guides me. The small rocks cause me to slip and slide a bit.

More than a couple of times I almost fall on my ass.

After a few minutes, we step inside a building, shielded from the biting wind.

No longer focusing all of my attention on trying to prevent a twisted ankle, I realize there was a conversation going on that just ended abruptly.

Because of me?

All at once my hackles rise and my chest constricts with panic.

I can't see them but I can feel them. The monsters in the darkness...

A door slams behind me and I nearly jump out of my skin.

The grip around my arm tightens, nudging me forward, then digs in deep when I don't budge.

I'm too frightened to keep moving.

My heels are trying to dig into the smooth floor while alarm bells go off inside my head.

"Be a good girl," the deep voice from earlier hisses as he drags me forward.

I'm already fucking up, I quickly realize. How the hell am I going to make it through this?

The fingers around my arm loosen and then I'm pushed backward, stumbling before I land on a chair.

Rattled, I shake my head a little and then my arms are yanked behind my back. My wrists slam together, and something is wrapped around them. Tightly binding them.

It all happens so quick, it's so damn efficient... they must have a lot of practice at this...

Beside me, someone groans in agony and it takes me a moment to realize it's Ivan.

Suddenly, the bag is yanked off my head and my eyes blur with tears as they adjust to the bright spotlight beaming down on me. I blink quickly to clear them.

Standing in front of me, with a smirk tugging at his lips, is the most beautiful man I've ever laid eyes on.

He's so beautiful, so unreal and ethereal, at first I think he must be a figment of my imagination. Blonde hair and blue eyes. Features so perfect I can find no flaw in them. The light seems to caress his glowing skin, but the longer and longer I look at him, the more I feel distressed.

He's too perfect... almost angelic.

But no angel would be in a place like this.

My eyes start to shy away from the beautiful man but then he steps forward, grabs a lock of my hair, and lifts it.

The smirk on his lips sharpens and he glances to my left.

I look over and gasp behind the tape covering my mouth. Ivan has been tied to a chair beside me, but his face is messed up. His right eye is swollen closed and his nose looks broken, bent crooked. And there's dried blood caking his nostrils and the tape covering his mouth.

"I could have sworn your wife was a blonde, Ivan," the beautiful man says with some amusement as his fingers rub my hair thoughtfully before dropping it.

Wife? Ivan is married?

You've got to be fucking kidding me...

My eyes narrow angrily at Ivan and the beautiful man tips his head back and laughs.

I ignore him, my anger momentarily overriding my good sense as his words repeat inside of my head.

All this time. All this *fucking* time Ivan has been pursuing me—stalking me and trying to control me—he's been married?!

Buying me things... Taking me out... Trying to sleep with me... When he already has a wife at home?

And he never mentioned it. No, I would have remembered that. I would have ended it immediately.

I wouldn't even be in this mess.

Fuck.

He's made me the other woman.

My stomach twists painfully and I feel like getting sick.

Laughter dying away, the beautiful man in front of me takes a step toward Ivan and reaches out, ripping the tape off that covers Ivan's mouth in one swift movement.

Ivan groans and I wince. That looked incredibly

painful, especially with all the dried blood that came off with the tape.

"Well?" our captor says with a bit of disgust, dropping the tape to the floor. "Do you have anything to say for yourself, Ivan?"

Ivan eyes our captor warily and then slowly shakes his head.

"Are you sure?" the beautiful man presses. "You don't even want to know why I've brought you here?"

Ivan takes in a breath, licks his bloodied lips, and then his eyes flick to me. "Why have you brought me here, Lucifer?"

Lucifer? This is the same Lucifer I hear Ivan talking about so often?

Lucifer grins and says with some satisfaction, "Well, with everything I've been hearing through the pipelines, I figured you had something you wanted to tell me."

Taking in Ivan's pale face and compressed lips, Lucifer scowls. "No? I was mistaken?"

Ivan's eyes dart around the room with a hint of desperation as if he's looking for an exit or way to escape this. I feel my own panic growing inside of my chest even though I don't really understand what's happening.

"Ah, well, if you have nothing to say, Ivan, I guess this was all just a waste of our time..."

Lucifer turns towards me and for a brief, glorious moment I truly believe this has all been a big misunderstanding and he's going to release me.

Then he reaches down, pulls a gun from his hip and presses it against my forehead.

The blood in my veins freezes and my heart stops beating.

I can't move, breathe, or blink.

I'm going to die. This beautiful man is going to blow my brains all over the concrete.

Thanks to Ivan, I'll never see my daughter again.

The weight of my life hanging in the balance is more than my mind can process. My thoughts race but everything around me begins to move in slow motion.

"No!" Ivan bellows and I watch the shadows behind Lucifer separate. A man steps forward, forming out of the darkness.

"No?" Lucifer repeats, sounding confused as he glances towards Ivan.

I can't look towards Ivan, my eyes are locked on the dark newcomer, drawn to him like a magnet. He takes a step forward, into the light, and for a hysterical second, I wonder if he means to save me as his hand drops to his hip.

But then his features come more into focus, and any hope I held withers inside of my heart.

The man looks so mean, so angry, his black eyes smoldering with such intense hatred as he glares at me, I realize he's probably just one of Lucifer's goons. Ready to back him up and shoot me dead if I somehow manage to escape the gun pressed against my head.

I hear Ivan clear his throat and say, "Perhaps there was something I wished to discuss with you..."

"Perhaps?" Lucifer repeats, incredulous. The barrel of the gun presses harder against my forehead and I whimper as it digs into my skin. "I don't have time for this shit..."

Lucifer's finger begins to move over the trigger and I squeeze my eyes shut, hoping it's quick.

"No! Wait!" Ivan cries out again. "There are many things I would like to discuss with you. Just don't hurt her..."

"What things?" Lucifer drawls out, sounding like he doesn't believe Ivan.

"Things regarding some mutual acquaintances of ours... from Japan.

I feel the gun pull away and my eyes pop open.

Lucifer's lips quirk up into a smirk and I see something flashing across his eyes. Satisfaction with a hint of amusement?

"Go on," he prompts Ivan.

There's a heavy pause and I watch Lucifer stiffen with irritation. He begins to lift the gun again, and my nose tingles painfully while spots dance in front of my eyes.

I don't know how much more I can take of this before I die of a heart attack.

"I want assurances that you won't kill me... or my mistress..."

"You're in no position to bargain."

"I know the person directly responsible for ordering the hit on your wife."

Lucifer laughs. "You do, do you?"

"Yes," Ivan says quickly. "I also know that there's to be another hit soon, on your children..."

The room, cold and silent up until now, feels like it explodes with a flurry of whispers and movements.

"Keep talking," Lucifer growls angrily. The gun drops away as he forgets about me and focuses all of his attention on Ivan.

"Only if you agree to my terms..." Ivan stammers.

Lucifer stiffens then his head turns towards me. His eyes, so bright, so cold now, I feel the full force of his anger and loathing.

If I were a bug, he would stomp me out of existence.

"Andrew," he snaps, and the man that formed in the shadows takes another step forward, into the light.

"Yes, sir?"

"Get rid of her," Lucifer orders and turns away.

Oh my god, he's not even going to do it himself. He just ordered his goon to kill me...

Eyes as black as a moonless night, the one Lucifer called Andrew glares murderously at me as he begins to approach me.

He's so big.

He's freakin' massive, I realize as he grows wider and taller, his feet eating up the distance between us.

Perhaps tonight has been just too much. My mind has cracked. Something inside of me must be broken.

Because I swear that even though Andrew is in the light now, the shadows from the corner have traveled with him.

And as he stops in front of me, reaching for me, those shadows wrap around me, seeping into my skin.

Vaguely, my brain registers four words, "Be a good girl," before my eyes roll into the back of my head.

4

ANDREW

Throwing the girl's body over my shoulder, I can't help but smirk at Ivan. Motherfucker thought he could get away with being silent with us. Thought he could be silent and get away from the shit pool he swam in.

Man looks like a little bitch now.

Standing in front of Ivan for a brief moment, I growl out, "Lucifer, if you need me for anything, let me know. I can take this piece of trash out too."

Lucifer laughs behind me. "No need for that just yet, Andrew, but I'll be sure to keep your offer in mind."

Slapping the girl's rump, I grin at Ivan. "See ya around, Ivan."

His face turns nearly purple as he yells at my back, "Don't you dare touch her!"

There's a loud crunch of fist meeting flesh.

Lucifer's dark laughter fills the darkness. "Don't worry

about her, Ivan. We have too many things to talk about right now."

Ivan better come to terms with what Lucifer is saying, his life depends on it.

And it seems that this little girl's does too.

Fucking shit, that sucks because she didn't seem too happy about learning that she's a mistress. It was obvious from the look on her face that she didn't know Ivan was married.

I walk out towards the waiting limousine we used to get here and open the passenger door. "Peter, take me to my car. I need to take care of our guest."

Pushing her still unconscious form across the seat, I get in beside her.

"Need me to call Harrold?"

"Nah, not yet at least. Seems Ivan is a bit sweet on this girl. Didn't want to play ball till she was threatened."

The car is moving onto a main road when Peter asks, "He talks because of a piece of ass?"

"Yeah, she's got a good juicy one too. But yeah, didn't say shit till Lucifer had a gun to her head."

Shaking my head, I think about her eyes, and how much terror and hatred for Ivan was in them.

The girl's body slowly stiffens up and I watch her breathing quicken. She must be coming to after she fainted.

Her breasts rise up and down in deep breaths now. And fuck if they don't look good. I can imagine my hands cupped around them, squeezing them.

The necklace I watched Ivan fasten around her neck is a bit tacky looking though. Looks like he's trying to compensate for something.

Fucker's probably got a small dick.

I can't remember a time when I had to do any of the things I saw him do with her tonight. I've never had to shower some chick with expensive shit just to keep her. My dick does a fine job of that on its own. I've also never had to grab a girl like he did in the restaurant and force her to get drunk to sleep with me. Shit, I've never even had to take advantage of a drunk woman.

Nah, they throw themselves at me, sober.

Watching her chest rise and fall, I feel just a hint of pressure down between my legs, my cock beginning to stir. It's been way too long since I've been between a woman's thighs.

Been at least a year.

Fuck, maybe longer than that. I've just been too busy ever since that shit went down with the Yakuza.

Since then Lucifer has done big things for our organization. He's increased the size of all of our holdings, as well as removed all of the Yakuza from Garden City. He's been rooting out anyone who had a hand in trying to kill his wife.

It's been tough to do too because what we originally thought was a two-sided war between us and the Japs has become a bit more tangled and complicated.

The Russians, while not directly involved, have been implicated in the mess. Not their soldiers themselves, but the cash they've been investing against us. There's nothing we can use as concrete proof against them... yet. Just rumors and whispers.

But if Ivan talks, it just might change all of that.

Ivan isn't one of the higher-ups with the Russians, but he's a top financier. He's not the type to get his hands dirty, though he has been behind quite a few solid dealings in Garden City. If there's been a big deal happening, you can usually find his name hidden in the details. He's the type of guy who likes to walk tall with the gangsters but keeps his name clean from the law. You won't find the Russian mafia tattoos on him, no, that would be too much for him.

That would actually take balls.

We first heard Ivan's name when we were interrogating the Yakuza after they kidnapped Lily. Again, there was nothing concrete. The leads we received didn't really amount to anything... until I took care of Bart.

Bart gave up some names to me before he died—Ivan being the top one of them. We've been watching the fucker for a while now, and waiting...

The roads are empty tonight, and as we pull up to the compound, I look back over to the pretending sleeping beauty. She's awake, trying to figure out what to do or what's going to happen next. I can tell just by the way she breathes, and the way her hands twitch even though she is trying to remain perfectly still.

Putting my lips right next to her ear, my nose fills with

the scent of her hair. It smells faintly of flowers and perspiration. She has been through some shit tonight.

"Do you remember what I told you before we got out of the car?" I ask in a low murmur only she can hear.

Her body locks up even further, but I see the smallest of nods from her head.

"Good, because I don't want you to be stupid. Be a good girl. Be smart," I say as I pull her tight to my body as we make a sharp turn.

Wrapping my arm around her, I hold her shoulders to my chest.

Her hands lace together as she tries to keep the shaking in her fingers from showing.

"Peter, park us right next to the car."

"Got it."

THE WIND IS BLOWING PRETTY HARD by the time I push her into the passenger seat of my BMW.

Leaning into the car, I brush her dark brown hair out of her face and look into her pale blue eyes. She's been crying, it's obvious from the mascara tracks running down her cheeks.

But she looks absolutely beautiful even when terrified.

Taking a corner of the silver duct tape that covers her mouth, I slowly peel it off. I can tell it's painful by the way she squints her eyes but she doesn't cry out from it or scream. There's a red patch of angry skin when the tape finally comes off.

Gesturing to her hands, I say, "The zip-ties stay on until we come to an understanding."

Grabbing the seatbelt, I bring it across her body and snap it into place. Pulling it tight, I say, "Don't move."

Shutting the door, I turn to Peter. "Have Harrold do something with the limo. No need to keep it around any longer."

"Got it. Anything else, Andrew?" he asks as he starts to pull his phone from his pocket.

"Not yet. I'll call you if I need anything."

Heading around my car, I feel my pocket vibrating before I even get to my door. Pulling it out, I see that it's Simon calling.

"Simon, how's it going?" I ask as I pull my door open and slide myself into the car.

"Lucifer told me about the complication," he says, not even bothering to answer my question.

Starting up the car, I put it into drive before I answer. "Yeah, intel got screwed up. We ended up with his mistress."

"Well, I have information about that little problem of yours."

"What do you mean problem of mine?" I ask as I look over at her.

Her eyes widen as she stares at me.

"She has a daughter."

"Fuck. Is it his?"

"No, I doubt it. She's five years old, named Abigail."

Looking over at the girl beside me, I force myself to call her a woman now. She doesn't look like she's had a kid, but then again what the fuck do I know about having kids?

"She's going to be your problem now, Andrew. The dirty face and sticky hands kind of problem."

I can hear him cringing through the phone.

Simon isn't one for kids, dirt, messes, loud laughter or anything fun really. He's also afraid of strip clubs. But being Lucifer's right-hand man means he's my boss.

That doesn't keep me from growling into the phone a few choice words at him.

"Abusing me is not going to change the matter, Andrew. Do you think Lucifer didn't see how you looked at the girl? He just called to make sure you were put in charge of the child. He thinks it will be good for your moral fiber."

"I fucking hate you, Simon," I grouse at him.

"She'll be delivered to your home in a couple hours. Johnathan will be picking her up from the babysitter."

"Simon, seriously, how the fuck did you find all this information out?"

"They call me the Spider for a reason, Andrew," he says as he disconnects the phone.

Fucking bastard. He's called the Spider alright because his web of information is vast as fuck. It's scary the shit he can find out.

Putting my phone down on the console, I growl out in

frustration. Where the fuck am I going to keep a kid at my house? I don't have toys and shit for a five-year-old.

Shaking my head at the problem, I give up on being able to change what is to come. There is no way I will be stepping back from a job Lucifer has handed me.

But fuck, a kid?

Looking over to the woman as we stop at a red light, I can see she wants to speak so badly but is doing her best to follow my rules.

Reaching over, I pat her thigh with my hand. Letting it rest there, I say quietly, "We need to have a talk, Amy."

Her eyes widen even further as she looks from my hand to my face. Stammering, she says, "Okay…"

"You're going to be staying with me for a while. Seems like your ex-boyfriend needs to work through some things with my boss."

"But… I… I can't. I have things… I have a…" Shaking her head, she tries to collect herself. "He's not my boyfriend, and I'm not his fucking mistress!"

"Not anymore you aren't," I snicker as pull us onto the highway.

"I mean I never was! We were dating for a couple of weeks, but… I… he just wouldn't take no for an answer."

I look at her again and I can see she's telling the truth, which sucks for her. Her value is dropping by the sentence right now.

"Well, right now that doesn't matter. Least not to me. You be a good girl like I said, and we will get along just fine."

She pulls away from my hand as she says, "I'm not a whore... You can't just make me sleep with you."

Laughing, I shake my head. "Nah, you'll want to do that on your own accord. I don't force women like that."

Snorting in derision, she says, "I so don't think that will be happening. Look, I have to go home. You can see I'm not a threat. I don't know what Ivan was about. There's nothing I can say that will hurt you guys."

"That's not going to be an issue. Look, Amy, things are going to happen now, whether you like it or not. You got involved with Ivan."

"How... How did you know my name?" she asks, and when I glance over she looks so pale it's like she's turned into a ghost.

"Same way I know Abigail's name."

We don't speak for a long while. Long enough for me to pull off the highway and head towards my small subdivision.

My house is in the newer section of Garden City, where all the well-to-dos do their daily commute from. It's not a bad house, pretty big for a single bachelor actually. I don't need three extra bedrooms, but for appearance's sake, I keep a home away from work.

Sometimes it feels good to come here and be normal.

We're pulling up to my driveway and turning in when Amy speaks again. "How... please don't hurt her. I'm begging you, she's a little girl. She doesn't even know of Ivan... Please."

When I pull to a stop inside of the garage, I look her

square in the eyes. "Don't worry about her. She'll be here in an hour or so, and she's as safe as can be. From us and from Ivan. So are you."

Getting out of the car, I go to her door and open it. After helping her out by the arm, I stand in front of her for a long time.

She's small compared to me, tiny really. Somewhere inside of myself I feel this odd desire to wrap her tight in my arms. I want to whisper words of comfort, but that shit won't work. She needs to know the truth of what's going on.

If she wasn't so damn ethereal and beautiful, I would just throw her in the closet and forget about her for a couple of weeks.

Reaching into my pocket, I pull out my folding knife. I snap it open in front of her and she lets out a small gasp.

Taking her hands, I slice through the zip tie.

Taking the cut zip tie with me, I turn away from her before I throw her over my shoulders and carry her off like some fucking caveman.

Fuck, I can't even explain it but I want to fucking *own* this woman. I want to carry her up to my bed and mark her and fuck her until she forgets she ever heard the name Ivan.

And I just might do that if I don't get a fucking grip on myself.

"You have a new reality, Amy. You can walk out of this house at any time, taking your daughter with you," I say as I open the door connecting the garage to the house.

Walking into the kitchen, I toss the zip tie in the garbage can, then head to the fridge for something cold and preferably alcoholic.

"What... What do you mean?"

Not looking at her, because then I'd want her lips, I say, "Exactly as I said. You can walk out that door right now. I won't hold you here."

It's obvious she's not all looks though when she asks, "What's the catch?"

"You will have the life expectancy of five hours. The Russians will be looking for you soon. They don't like it when one of their rich boys go missing. They will find you, then they will ask you questions you don't have answers to. When you can't tell them what they want to know, they'll get rid of you. If you're lucky, they'll put you down like an old horse. But more than likely they'll sell you off to a slave ring."

She lets out a very quiet sigh as she asks, "Or?"

Turning to her, I hold out a bottle of beer. "You and Abigail stay here with me. Under my protection."

She shakes her head at the beer. I shrug and put it back in the fridge. Closing the fridge, I pop the top of my bottle and set it on the counter to take off my suit jacket.

"What, like your sex slave?"

Growling, I say, "I don't use women like that. I've said that already, and I hate repeating myself."

"What happens when your boss, Lucifer, doesn't want us around anymore?"

"You'll be mine, so that won't happen."

Growling right back at me, she says, "I'm not anyone's!"

"We'll see," I say as I leave the kitchen. Then I shout over my shoulder, "I wouldn't bother running to your aunt's. That's the first place anyone would check."

5

AMY

The man from the shadows, the man Lucifer called Andrew, walks into his living room, sits down on his couch, and flips on his TV like it's the most normal thing in the world. He kicks his feet up, propping them up on his coffee table, and leans back, taking a deep drink from his beer.

From the kitchen, I watch with dismay as he lifts his remote and starts flipping through channels.

Shaking my head, I try to clear it.

I've stepped into the Twilight Zone... That's the only thing that makes sense.

An hour ago, I was in a dark, grimy warehouse with that man and my life was in peril. Now we're here, in this perfectly normal looking house, and he's drinking a beer while watching the sports channel.

I don't even know how to begin coping with this.

I could try to make a run for it. Looking towards the

door, it's tempting as hell. My hand longs to reach for the handle, my fingers ache to twist it open to freedom.

And he's not even bothering to keep me from doing it.

But then, that only makes his earlier warning seem that much more legit.

No doubt he's not trying to prevent me from leaving because he was being completely honest.

I'm a dead woman if I walk out that door. I'm trapped here with him.

Unless that's just what he wants me to believe...

Fuck. What do I do? Do I risk it?

Unable to bring myself to join him in front of the TV, I pace back and forth in his kitchen, trying to come up with a plan. There has to be a way to get Abigail and I out of this mess.

But even if I were able to get us away, where would we go? They already know about my aunt, and she's the only family I have. I do have a little bit of money saved up, but it's not much. After Ivan got me fired from my job because I used it as an excuse to avoid going out with him, I've had a hell of a time trying to find another position.

We could make a run for Mexico... but with the cartels there, we're probably better off heading for Canada. I could rent a car and ditch it as soon as we make it across the border but then what? I don't exactly have the connections to start over. We would need new identities and the papers to go with them.

Fuck, I don't even have our real identities. I don't have

my purse or my wallet, and I have no idea where I left them.

Coming to a stop, I lean against the wall and have the strongest urge to bang my head against it. I feel so stupid for getting myself in this mess. I feel so stupid for being flattered by Ivan's attention.

Men have caused me nothing but trouble. You'd think after Abigail's father left us high and dry I would have learned from my mistake.

I'm not sure how long I lean against the wall, trying to keep my shit together. But as soon as I hear the door opening behind me, I whip around to face whoever is coming through it.

"Mommy!" Abigail cries out and rushes over to me.

Wrapping my arms around my little girl instantly makes me feel a little better. Bending down, I hug her tightly until she wiggles her way out of my arms.

"Johnathan," Andrew says, standing from the couch and nodding his head at the man that came in behind Abigail.

I glance towards Johnathan and then have to do a double take. If he wasn't so gigantic and fierce looking, he'd look absurd. With his long, dirty blonde hair and tattoos all over his neck and hands, he looks like someone squeezed a grungy biker into a designer black suit.

Johnathan scowls and thrusts out his arm, and that's when I notice he's holding out Abigail's *Beauty and the Beast* backpack.

"This came with *it*," he rumbles.

Andrew frowns at the backpack like he doesn't know what to do with it. The two men then seem to have a stare off before Johnathan shrugs and opens his hand, letting the backpack fall to the floor.

"Mommy," Abigail says, tugging on my hand to get my attention.

"Yes, sweetie?" I ask, tearing my eyes away from the two menacing men as they talk quietly to each other.

Abigail beams up at me. "Johnny let me have chocolate ice cream for dinner."

"What?" I blink down at her.

Johnathan grumbles and stops talking to Andrew to turn an accusing eye on my daughter. "You weren't supposed to tell anyone."

I frown at him and start to step in front of her, not liking the way he's looking at her or talking to her.

Abigail pops her head out from behind me though and then says cheerfully, "He also let me have some coke."

"What?!" I snap. Did I just hear that right?

Johnathan takes a nervous step back and throws his hands up. "I only gave it to her to get her to stop crying."

"You gave my daughter coke to calm her down?!" I repeat incredulously.

"He told me *only two sips* but I really liked it, Mommy, so I drank the whole the can!"

I shake my head in disbelief. She's going to be up all night. Even now she's struggling to stay still. She bounces on her toes beside me and then her eyes widen as she takes in the house.

She tries to pull away from me to explore, but I grab her by the hand and tug her close.

I haven't forgotten for a second what kind of men these two are.

Abigail keeps tugging on me though and eventually I give in. Using my hand to drag me behind her, she darts around Andrew's house, taking everything in.

"Johnny told me we were going to be staying with Andrew for awhile," she babbles happily as she leads me over to a bookcase.

"He did, did he?" I groan. "What else did Johnny tell you?"

Instead of telling me, she comes to an abrupt stop and then blinks up innocently at me. "Is Andrew your new boyfriend, Mommy?" she asks, her big blue eyes full of twinkling innocence.

"Good god, no," I exclaim immediately, and take a deep breath to get over the shock of the question.

"Okay!" Abigail says cheerfully, completely unfazed by my reaction, and tugs me over to the TV.

I don't know how she does it, she must have some sixth sense when it comes to televisions, but she picks up his remote off the table and is able to flip through his channels until she finds a cartoon she wants to watch.

I watch her become engrossed in the cartoon and I can't explain how I feel.

I'm happy Abigail is fine and doesn't realize something bad is happening, but I'm also scared out of my wits. I'm terrified that I won't be able to protect her from whatever is going to happen here.

She's so young, completely oblivious, and totally vulnerable.

If they kill me, what will happen to her?

The cold spike of terror that slices through me is so strong I almost drop to my knees. Heart hammering behind my ribs, I push that thought out of my head. If I keep thinking like that I'll never figure out a good way to get us out of this.

I decide to take a seat on the couch while she chooses to stand in front of it, bouncing up and down.

In front of the door, Andrew and Johnathan continue to talk quietly, scowling at each other. I try to watch them inconspicuously, dividing my attention between them and Abigail, but I learn nothing new.

I wish I could hear what they're discussing but I can't hear anything over Abigail's cartoon.

Finally, after a few more minutes, Johnathan leaves and Andrew disappears into the kitchen before reappearing with a fresh beer. Picking Abigail's backpack off the floor, he carries it over to me, and my muscles tense up as he drops it at my feet.

I half expect him to try to take a seat beside me but after a moment he turns away and walks over to a recliner. Dropping down into the recliner, I feel his dark eyes glaring at me as he leans back and drinks his beer.

Keeping my eyes focused forward, it's everything I can do to keep from peeking over at him.

How do I get us out of this mess? How do I get us to safety?

Without my wallet, escape feels impossible. But there must be another way... there must be something I didn't think of.

If I had access to my money, if I could make it to the bank, we wouldn't even need to drive all the way to Canada. We'd only need to make it to the airport. We could hop on a plane and go anywhere...

But I would need our passports.

Fuck, getting away feels like an impossible feat.

Feeling Andrew's eyes boring into me, I slowly turn my head to look at him. Jaw clenched and eyes narrowed, he stares at me with what looks like unabashed loathing.

I don't know what I did to deserve to earn such hatred. He said he would protect us, but he must be thinking twice about it now.

"She asleep?" Andrew asks gruffly, yanking me out of my thoughts.

Glancing down, I see that Abigail has curled up beside me into a little ball.

She must have crashed from all the sugar Johnathan gave her.

Looking up at Andrew, I nod my head at him. He sets his bottle down and stands from the recliner. Walking over to us, I feel myself tensing up, not sure what he means to do.

He bends down and I pull back, retreating into the cushions of the couch.

His dark eyes lock on mine as if daring me to do something and then he picks up Abigail's sleeping form.

My heart jumps into my throat and I immediately hate seeing her in his arms. Cradled in his hold, she looks so vulnerable, so fragile. I reach out but he takes a step back before I can grab her.

She doesn't even realize the danger she's in. Murmuring, she snuggles up to him and his arms tighten protectively around her.

"I can carry her..." I protest.

He completely ignores me.

"Follow me and I'll show you to your room," he says, turning away and walking off.

Jumping up from the couch, I grab her backpack and follow closely on his heels.

Every little anxious nerve in my body is sounding off. He said we were under his protection, but does that protection extend to him?

He leads me up a carpeted flight of stairs and down a short hall with four doors.

Stopping in front of the third door, he nods at me, expecting me to open it. Twisting the knob, I push the door open but don't walk in until he does.

He carries Abigail into the room and heads for the big bed taking up the middle. I watch with my heart in my throat as he gently lowers her down.

Straightening from the bed, he stares down at her for a moment before turning to me.

I don't know why but there's this sudden tension between us. His face hardens and somehow, he looks even angrier than before.

A shiver runs down my spine as he stares me down.

He takes a step toward me and I bring up Abigail's backpack, using it as a shield.

For the first time tonight I watch his face soften and his lips curve into a smile.

"Goodnight, Amy. I'll see you in the morning," he says, brushing past me and walking out the door.

I expel a breath I didn't realize I was holding then quickly close the door behind him. Pushing in the lock, I finally feel like I can relax a little.

Getting my pulse back under control, I turn around and take in the room. A king-sized bed takes up most of the middle, flanked by two nightstands. The headboard of the bed is pushed up against the right wall, while a tall, cherry wardrobe is up against the left wall. Against the back wall is the only window.

I walk up to the window and yank open the curtains then try the window. It opens easily and I slide up the screen to poke my head out.

The street is quiet. The occasional cold gust of wind rattling the naked trees is the only sound.

Looking down, my heart sinks as I realize it's too high of a drop for Abigail. I might be able to survive it but there's absolutely nothing to break our fall. The side of the house is made up of smooth beige siding. There's nothing for us to use for climbing down.

Abigail murmurs in her sleep and I pull my head back in, glancing towards her. She shivers and burrows deeper into the covers.

With a sigh of resignation, I pull the screen back down and close the window.

Even if I were able to fasten a rope out of the sheets, it just feels too risky. Abigail would probably get hurt. If I try to shimmy down while holding her, we'd probably both break our necks.

Walking over to her, I slide her shoes off and tuck her under the thick, fluffy comforter. It's not until I slide into the bed beside her and lay my head down on the pillow that I feel a little pinch around my neck.

Glancing down, I look at the necklace Ivan gave me with a frown. With everything going on, I totally forgot about it.

Sitting up, I unclasp the necklace then let the strands of diamonds slide through my fingers to pool into my palm. There's a sickening amount of diamonds. I knew when Ivan locked it around my neck that he expected repayment... in bed.

Cupping the diamonds in my hand, I watch them sparkle in the moonlight and feel a warm burst of hope.

Who needs a purse or a wallet when I have this? Even if I only get a fraction of what they're really worth, it will be more than enough for us to get away...

All I have to do is get us to a pawn shop.

6
AMY

Tossing and turning, I try my hardest to fall asleep. After about an hour, I give up, accepting that it's just not going to happen.

I've been through too much tonight and my brain won't stop replaying it over and over again. I keep reliving Ivan's cold touch. Andrew's smoldering eyes.

And Lucifer pointing a gun at my head.

Sliding my hand under my pillow, I check to make sure my necklace is still where I left it. Then I sit up. Carefully, I pull the blanket back without disturbing Abigail and slide out of bed.

My feet hit the floor and my toes sink into the plush carpet as I stand.

I take a moment to tuck the blanket around Abigail and resist the urge to smooth her hair back.

Quietly, I tiptoe my way across the room and open the door.

The hallway is pitch black. I pause for a moment, hoping my eyes will adjust to the dark, but every light in the house must be off.

I can't see my own hand in front of my face, and I should probably just go back to bed, but it feels like some unseen force is tugging me, urging me to step into the dark.

Pressing my palm against the wall, I use touch to guide me down the hall. Carefully, I slide my foot forward, ensuring the floor is there before I move.

I focus so much attention on walking that I don't realize I'm not alone.

I make it to the next door when I'm suddenly grabbed.

"Where are you going?" Andrew growls.

Grabbing me roughly, he spins me around and pins me against the wall.

So terrified I can't scream, only gasp, my world spins and my eyes strain against the darkness, trying to make out his face.

It's so dark I can't see him, only feel him.

His warmth.

His angry energy.

His menace.

"Are you trying to run away?" he asks harshly, his hands tightening around my wrists and pinching my skin.

"N—n—no," I stammer, my heart beating wildly

behind my ribs. Of course it would look that way but, "I couldn't sleep."

"So?" he rumbles ominously and takes a step forward, pressing me into the wall with his chest.

The length of his hard body presses against my body and alarm bells start going off inside of my head as he cages me in.

One wrong word and this could be it...

"I... I just wanted to get a drink of water," I squeak, trying to ignore how warm he feels.

Seriously, he's burning hot. The heat from his chest is scorching my breasts through my dress.

"Is that all?" he asks, his voice softening, and his fingers start to loosen around my wrists.

Thinking we've cleared up the little misunderstanding, I start to relax a little and take a moment to catch my breath before answering, "Yes."

"You weren't..." His knee nudges at my knees. "Trying to find your way to my room?"

"Of course not!" I gasp and lock my knees together, denying him entrance.

What the hell is he doing?

He pulls on my wrists suddenly, yanking them up, and stretching me out on the wall like I'm on a vertical rack.

I can't squeeze my legs together stretched out on my tiptoes like this.

His knee spreads my knees easily now and then he's

fitting himself between my thighs. I'm so shocked, so disturbed, I freeze up, unsure of what to do.

Will he hurt me if I fight him? Or is he counting on my submission?

Warm breath caresses my face, stroking over my nose, my cheeks, and then puffs against my lips.

"That's a shame," he states softly.

The darkness seems to shimmer around us. I stare hard, wishing I could see his face. Wishing I had more than just the sound of his voice to go on.

"It is?" I ask tentatively, hoping I'm mistaken and he's not meaning what I think he's meaning.

"Yes," he says huskily, his voice deepening.

"H...h...how so?"

"Because I want you."

I jerk as if he just hit me and feel a spike of desire slam into my core. He wants me? Why does that revelation both frighten and excite me?

God, I'm so fucked up.

The longer he presses against me, the more I'm physically responding to it. My nipples tighten and tingle against the press of his chest.

His hips lock against my hips and then my core clenches as I feel a hard bulge pressing against my mons.

"Please," I groan, trying to arch away from him. Trying to escape the intense sensation. "Don—"

His mouth covers my mouth, smothering the rest of my plea.

I start to struggle now but it's too little, too late. I've already allowed myself to be lured into the trap.

I try to twist my face away. I try to rip my wrists free from his grip. But the more I fight him, the more it seems to turn him on.

The more the snare tightens.

His huge body crushes me against the wall.

"Fuck, you taste so good," he moans before his tongue sweeps into my mouth.

His tongue touches my tongue and all the little nerves in my body light up in response.

Why do I like this? Why do I want to pull him closer instead of pushing him away?

Is it because it's been so long since I've been touched? Or is it because I can't see him in the dark?

I don't know. All I know is that I feel like I've been barely treading water and now I'm being pulled under the surface.

I'm drowning in sensation.

In his warmth. In his presence.

His mouth slants over my mouth, over and over. With each pull, with each suckle, I feel like I lose a little more of myself.

He's breaking me down, kiss by kiss.

And before I know it, I'm kissing him back.

My tongue desperately seeks out his tongue. My body strains and stretches towards his body.

I arch and moan into his mouth.

He rolls his hips forward, his trapped erection grinding against my clit.

Logic, reason, and conscious thought are all lost, replaced by a need I've never felt with Ivan. My brain is being lulled into a false sense of security by the slow building throb.

It could all be merely a survival reflex but I can't seem to stop.

After being so close to death, I just want to *live*.

Something buried deep inside of me wants this.

I have the strongest desire to be joined with him. To be beneath him.

"Amy," he groans, and to hear him say my name like that makes me feel so strong, so powerful. "Wrap your legs around me."

I shouldn't. This is insane.

"Amy," he growls when I don't instantly obey.

And that growl, god, it does things to me.

Wicked, sinful things.

Andrew, he's not a good man. I have no delusions about that. And what he's doing to Abigail and me, there's really no excuse for it.

But he wants me, and it feels so good to be wanted.

My knees shake and my arms ache in this stretched out position. If I had any sense, I'd try to get away...

Not wrap my legs around him. Not give in to the moment.

But fuck it, I'm *living* in this moment.

I could be dead tomorrow.

If this is my last night on Earth, at least I'll be in the arms of a beautiful, dangerous man.

And if he's ordered to kill me... well, maybe just maybe he'll think twice about it.

I wrap my legs around his waist.

Releasing my wrists, his arms snake around my back. His hands grab my ass and he hefts me up. Then he spins us around and I'm grabbing him.

I cling to him as he carries me through the dark hall, into a dark room, and lowers me down on something soft.

Now that we're in a bed, all bets seem to be off.

His hands grab at my dress, yanking it up and over my head. My hands grab at his shirt, my clumsy fingers fumbling with his buttons for a moment before I decide to just tear it open.

I hope that shirt was expensive.

With a chuckle, his hands slide behind me and he unsnaps my bra. Then his mouth covers my mouth, his kiss hungry and desperate as he pushes my bra down and cups my breasts with his big hands.

Groaning, I arch into his grip, squirming against the bed. All thoughts of removing the rest of his clothing forgotten.

He squeezes me, his thick fingers wrapping around me. Constricting me with the most delicious pressure.

I cry out, throwing my head back as my core clenches, hard.

Taking his sweet time, he plays with me. His hands molding me, reshaping me.

Driving me insane.

And just when I think I can stand no more, he covers my nipple with his wet hot mouth.

"Andrew," I gasp as he starts to suckle hungrily, melting in his arms.

Turning his head from side to side, he lavishes each breast, worshipping them with his lips, teeth, and tongue.

Then he begins to push me down.

My limbs weak, I go down easily, unable to put up much a fight.

His mouth leaves my breasts, kissing a wet path down my stomach.

As he slides my panties down my hips, and the cool air hits my wet sex, I try to sit up in alarm.

"Amy," he growls and pushes me back down.

I thought I wanted to do this but now that we've gotten to this point I'm not so sure...

My panties slide over my ankles and then he spreads my legs wide.

"Wait..." I cry out but he ignores me.

Grabbing me by the hips, I feel his breath against my thigh and then his tongue is sliding through my folds.

"Oh god," I groan, my hips trying to jerk out of his hands.

"No," he growls angrily and takes another swipe at my folds.

"Fuck," I whimper, almost bucking him off as his tongue slides up and down.

My pulse is pounding so hard I'm seeing stars.

Then his mouth completely covers my clit and I lose it. Suckling just like he did on my breasts, his mouth pulls on my clit, bringing me just to the brink of orgasm.

Then his mouth goes slack.

"What?!" I cry out in dismay, and feel him chuckle against my swollen, sensitive flesh. "Why did you stop?"

He pushes up from the bed, looming above me in the darkness.

I blink my eyes, and much to my dismay they start to adjust to the dark. There's just enough light coming through a window to light him up.

I watch him unbuckle his pants and then shove them down. "If you want to come, you'll have to come on my cock."

He shoves his boxer briefs down and then the biggest, thickest cock I've ever laid eyes on springs upwards.

Gulping, I stare at him and then slowly begin to crawl backward.

I've made a mistake. A very *big* mistake.

If he tries to thrust that thing inside of me he's going to split me in half.

Reaching down, he grabs me by the ankles and drags me back down the bed. "Where do you think you're going?"

"I...I..." I stammer, trying to think up a good excuse.

"You're not afraid, are you, Amy?" he grins down at me.

I shake my head at the same time my hands come up, pushing on his chest as he comes down on top of me.

He covers me, his weight heavy and solid.

"Good," he says, grabbing up my hands. His fingers slide through my fingers, squeezing almost tenderly, before he pins them above my head. "Because I would never hurt you."

"You won't hurt me?" I blink up at him in surprise.

Slowly, he shakes his head.

How does that make any sense?

Before I can question him further, he bends down and presses a wet kiss against my lips.

Fingers tightening around my fingers, the rest of his weight comes down, crushing me against the bed.

His leg slides between my legs, spreading me open. Then something thick and hard pushes against my sex.

"Wait," I mumble into his mouth. "I'm not on any birth control..."

"Good," he groans and pushes forward.

Inch by slow inch, he eases himself inside, filling me up.

Oh my god.

He's so damn big... if I wasn't already soaking wet he would have split me wide open.

"Fuck, you're tight," he grunts, bottoming out.

I'm so full, so overwhelmed, I can't respond.

Voice strained, he remarks, "You feel like a fucking virgin."

He begins to slide out, and the sensation is so sharp, so strong, I want to beg him to stop.

But then he pushes back in and all I want to do is beg him to do it again.

"How long has it been, Amy?"

I shake my head. I don't want to talk right now, I just want to *feel*.

In and out, he glides. Stretching me. Touching every little sensitive spot inside of me.

Reawakening my aching throb with a vengeance.

"Amy," he growls. "I asked you a question..."

Deeper and deeper he pushes, my body beginning to adjust to the sheer size of him.

"How long," he grunts, his teeth nipping my bottom lip.

"Years," I groan. Amazed I could get that much out.

"How many years?" he presses, slamming forward and grinding himself against my clit.

Trapped beneath his weight, I writhe and squirm against the bed as he uses his body to drive me to the brink of blissful madness.

Then, just as my orgasm is within reach, he stops.

"How many years, Amy?"

Desperate for my release, I clench down on him and cry out, "Four or five! I don't know! Before Abigail was born."

"Good girl," he grunts and starts pounding his cock inside me like he's trying to pound me through the bed.

And then, quite suddenly, I'm tumbling over the edge of my release and shattering into a million pieces.

My fingers squeeze his fingers, aching to grab him. Aching to sink my nails into his skin.

Muscles locking up, my insides melt and I feel like I'm gushing all over him.

"Oh fuck," he cries out in surprise. "Oh fuck, oh fuck," he repeats over and over again as my pussy spasms, milking him.

Sucking him in.

A moment later he roars and I'm filled with the most delicious warmth.

Grinding his cock deep, he pours himself inside of me until he has nothing left to give. Then he collapses on top of me.

Spent.

Crushed beneath his weight, I begin to struggle for air. Sensing my distress, he rolls off of me, giving me room to breathe.

Side by side, we stare up at the ceiling, panting as we catch our breath.

The euphoria of the orgasm begins to wear off. Reality comes crashing back in.

Did I really just do that?

I glance over at him.

Yep, I just did that.

Fuck.

Panicking, I start to jump up but he must have anticipated it. Grabbing me, he drags me close and wraps his arms around me like a vise.

"Where do you think you're going?" he asks gruffly, trapping me against his side.

"I was going to return to my room…"

"This is your room now."

"But…"

"No buts, Amy," he says, his arms tightening around me. "You made your choice. You're mine now."

7

ANDREW

It's the pitter-patter of little feet slapping quietly against the hard wood floors of the hallway that wakes me out of a dead sleep. I don't have anything in this house that would make that type of noise. No children, no pets.

Then again, the warm body draped across my chest begs to differ.

Her leg is so tightly wrapped around mine that I feel like I've been wrapped up by a boa constrictor. It's a silky-smooth leg at that. The kind of leg that is graceful, yet has underlying muscle to it.

Fuck, just the thought of her leg is making my morning erection feel like a steel log sticking straight up.

The feet pass outside my door as they head towards the stairs. Amy isn't stirring though, if anything she looks like she's dead to the world. That tends to happen when I put a woman through her paces twice in one night.

I wanted to try for a third go of things this morning when we woke up, but it looks like that's not going to happen.

Gently removing her head from my shoulder, I slide my leg out from under hers at the same moment.

The dawn light coming through the window gives me the opportunity to see how amazingly beautiful she is. She's had a rough night, no doubt about that, but here, sleeping in my bed with her makeup messed up, hair everywhere, and a small bite mark on her shoulder from last night, she's fucking gorgeous.

Fuck me. I've never seen a woman as attractive as she is right now in my life. I can only imagine how much better it will be when she is showered and fresh.

Fuck, just thinking about that keeps my dick hard. I really need to master the fucker before he stays like this for good.

Every part of her last night begged for me to take her, to take control. Some primal instinct reared its head inside of me. The bite on her shoulder was a small mark, but it's something I know she will see in the mirror. I want her to see it.

Fuck, I want the world to see it. She's mine now.

Grabbing a pair of jeans from the dresser and a t-shirt, I throw them on quickly and head out of the room to find the wayward imp.

Heading back the way she came, I see her little brown head bobbing up and down to some song she is singing to herself as she climbs up the stairs.

"Hey Abigail," I say quietly to her.

Her head snaps up with a small gasp and she squeaks out, "Where's my mommy? Is Johnathan here?"

Motioning for her to follow me, I say, "No, he went home last night, and your mother is in her bedroom. Want to see where it is?"

Nodding her head, she follows me as I lead her to my bedroom.

Opening the door quietly, I point to the sleeping beauty in my bed. "She had a rough night last night. I think we should let her get some good rest."

Leading Abigail downstairs to the kitchen, I'm sitting her down at the table for some breakfast when her little lip starts to quiver. She looks like a little replica of Amy, except this little one is on the verge of tears.

Fuck. I don't do tears.

"What's wrong, princess?"

"My Molly is at home. She didn't get to sleep in my bed last night."

Well, fuck. In for a penny, in for a pound, I guess. Taking her mom as mine means I take her too. Fuck... Girl needs a doll or some shit, then she's going to get it.

"Oh, that's a pretty serious issue isn't it?"

Nodding her head solemnly, she says, "She gets real scared and sad if I'm not home with her."

Damn, just hearing about the doll brings up a very big problem for me. We don't have any clothes here for either of them and if I plan on keeping them both I need to fix that.

I pull my cellphone from my pocket. Scrolling through my contacts, I need to figure out how to get the doll and some clothes for them.

Looking over at my little princess, I can see that little lip quivering again. Shit, I need the kid on my side of the fence. I want her mommy too much to let a doll get in the way of things.

"Would you want a new Molly?" I ask, and even as the words come out of my mouth I can see her eyes getting a little glassy from the emotions ready to burst out.

"No...that... no, my Molly needs me."

Nodding my head, I push the call button on Johnathan. "I promise she will be here before bedtime then. Sound good, princess?"

Her eyes light up at that. "Oh, yes!"

"What the fuck are you calling me for?" Johnathan growls loudly into the phone.

Glancing at the clock on the stove, I do notice it's a bit early. "I got a job for you?"

"Fuck, what is it? This a job from Lucifer? I'm supposed to be off for a couple of days."

Shit, that's right. Still, he's one of the guys I trust the most to get a shit job done.

"Five large to do a pickup."

"What the fuck do you want me to grab?" he asks, and I can tell he's getting clear-headed.

"I need you to—"

He interrupts me before I get to finish. "Fuck it, dude. You pulled me into a job last night a half hour after I got off an eighteen-hour flight. I'm fucking drained and need to sleep."

"Six large and get the fuck up, asshole. It's a simple job, and one I can call on the higher power to have assigned if I need it to be."

"Seriously? Fuck, this better be good, Andrew."

"I need you to go to the girl's house and grab clothes for them. Then I need you to go to Abigail's bedroom, there's a little..."

I trail off as I hear Johnathan muttering very dark words about my parentage.

Smiling at Abigail, I ask, "Exactly who is Molly, princess?"

"She's my panda!"

"Grab one Molly the Panda bear from the bed. Get some clothes of hers too... anything else, Abigail?"

"She likes her pink umbrella!" she giggles as she goes back to placing her silverware by her plate.

Sitting there so prim and proper like, she looks like a little cartoon princess. Big blue eyes, chocolate brown hair, and fair skinned.

"Get Molly's pink umbrella too."

The mutterings of my parentage have changed to my empty brain capacity.

"Have James drive you too, and keep an eye out. I'm thinking there's going to be some serious heat around the apartment."

Instantly he stops his muttering.

I can hear a grin in his voice as he asks, "What kind of heat are we talking?"

"Russian kind. We borrowed one of their big backers. The guy was sweet on Amy."

"Hmph, should I expect a welcome party?"

"Probably. But I want you to keep this as quiet as possible. If there are any obstacles, you need to get rid of them. I want this quiet, ghostly fucking quiet."

"Got it. I'll take Peter instead, he's better at the quiet job types. Fucker would be a hell of a cat burglar."

"Sounds good. I want it all before bedtime."

"Dude, you sound like such a pussy."

"Fuck you, biker-boy-asshole."

He hangs up his phone and I only realize my side of the conversation wasn't so quiet when I turn around to see Abigail's eyes go wide.

We stare at each other for a moment and then she says....

"I'm hungry, Andrew. That ice cream was yummy last night; do you have any?"

Laughing at her big blue puppy dog eyes, I shake my head. "Sorry kiddo, no ice cream here. I have stuff for breakfast though if you feel like you would want some of that."

We're about halfway through breakfast when I hear feet running across the upstairs. A second later, I hear them coming down the stairs.

"Your mother is awake," I announce to Abigail as Amy

comes to a screeching halt in the kitchen. She looks wide-eyed at both me and the little girl.

"Hi, Mommy!" Abigail giggles as she jumps out of her chair and races to hug her mom.

Hugging her daughter tight to her side, Amy looks at me with worried eyes. "What have you two been up to?"

"Andrew made me pancakes and bacon! Lots of milk, too!"

Tugging away from her mom, Abigail grabs Amy's hand and pulls her to our table.

Grinning at Amy, I point to the plate I set for her. "Yeah, you missed out on our early breakfast. But I can make you some too if you want."

As soon as Abigail slips from the table and shoots off to the couch for her morning cartoons, I stand up from my place at the table. Amy hasn't moved from her spot near where Abigail was sitting. She looks pissed and scared at the same time.

I see the fight in her but I can tell she genuinely fears for her life. She has a right to be both, but not with me. I would never do anything to hurt her or Abigail, they're mine now.

Standing up from the table, I walk over to Amy. I take her by the hand and she stands up hesitantly. Abigail can see us from the living room and I think right now we need a bit of privacy.

Leading Amy to the counter area of the kitchen, out of Abigail's sight, I give her a good once over. She looks far too good in just a long t-shirt.

"What we did last night," she hisses at me with an angry look. "You totally took advantage... I... we can't do that again."

Snickering, I cross my arms over my chest. "That's not what you said when I stuck my tongue in your—"

Her eyes go wide and her face flushes a bright red. "I'm so never allowing you to—"

Grabbing her by the hips, I pull her into my body. She isn't wearing a bra right now, and as soon as I press her to me, her hard nipples press into my chest.

Leaning down, I cover her mouth with mine and turn us toward the counter. Lifting her up, I set her down on top of it and push my hips between her legs.

She's as resistant to letting me between her thighs as she is in kissing me back. I don't stop though; I know what she needs. It's like that old saying, her lips are saying no but those eyes are saying *fuck yes*.

Slowly her hands stop beating at my chest. They latch around my neck and her mouth opens. Her tongue comes out, tentative at first, before meeting me lick for lick.

I can feel the warmth of her pussy pushing against my jeans and I can barely contain my desire to claim her right here, right now.

Two things keep me from unzipping my pants and thrusting myself deep inside her tight pussy. A giggling little princess behind me and my phone suddenly ringing.

Pulling my lips away from Amy's, I growl. "Shit."

Turning around, I stare at a laughing Abigail. "I'm going to get you, little princess!"

"Mommy said you weren't her boyfriend, but you are! You are!"

"Oh god..." I hear Amy mutter behind me.

Pulling my phone from my pocket, I look down.

Fuck.

Pushing connect, I look back up to Amy. "Gotta take this, babe, but I'll be back."

"Please tell me you aren't calling me babe now, Andrew," Lucifer says in a quiet voice.

"No sir, that would be someone else," I say.

"Good. Though if you are calling the young lady I charged you with taking care of last night, babe..." he trails off and for the life of me I have absolutely no clue what his tone is.

Because right now I'm in foreign waters. I've never been in a position like this before, and I really don't know how he's going to handle me claiming Amy as mine.

Honesty with Lucifer is always the best way to go though. "Yes, sir, I am."

There's a very long, pregnant pause. Like two minutes of silence. No breathing, no mutterings, no anything. I'm half tempted to say something, but I keep my peace.

Anything I say now just sounds like excuses.

I glance over at Amy and I can tell she knows who I'm speaking to. Her body is rigid and her previous blushing skin is pale white.

Pulling the phone away from my mouth, I grab her by

the back of the neck. Pushing my lips right next to her ear, I murmur quietly, "Mine."

She looks from me to the phone twice before she quietly hops down from the counter. "I'm going to go play with Abigail for a bit. Give you some privacy."

Nodding my head, I wait for Lucifer to finally speak. "You do know I could go without these kind of complications, these kinds of headaches."

Laughing, I say, "Life isn't fun for you, Lucifer, without this kind of thing. You'd be bored stiff."

"How serious is this, Andrew?"

"How serious were you?" I don't need to say Lily's name; he knows what I am talking about.

"Very well. But we need to talk about your timing some time."

"Probably... nothing I can do about it though."

"Probably," he sighs. "So this is why when I called Johnathan to get a report about his most recent trip I find out he's already on a job for you with Peter?"

"Yeah, my girls need some of their personal assets and Molly the Panda."

"What is Molly the Panda?"

"Abigail's panda bear."

"Please tell me you will be taking pictures of Johnathan holding that?"

"Like I could stop myself."

"Sounds good. He will be keeping this a simple job, I hope? The Russians have to have an idea of what happened to Ivan by now. But I don't want to leave a giant calling card."

"It will be a quick grab. I think it will also give us a chance to find out who's watching her place and how far they want to take things. They have to be careful right now, they can't be seen going on full defense. Nothing is really known beyond Ivan was snatched, and why would they blame us... We're their *friends,* right?"

"Sounds good, keep me abreast of it all."

"Will do."

"Is there anything you need for them to be more comfortable?"

"No, I think we're good for right now. I'm going to take them shopping tomorrow for clothes and toys. I want them to feel at home."

"Hmm. Why don't you come out to the compound with your girls tomorrow night for dinner? We can have a talk while the wives get to know each other."

Well, fuck. Looks like Amy and I just got hitched by the devil himself.

Fuck, did I just get a readymade family? I think I did. It's not like I didn't already claim her as mine... this just makes it real.

"Yes, sir. I'll see you there."

Disconnecting the call, I set the phone down on the counter. That went better than I could have possibly hoped for.

Turning towards the living room, I go searching for my princess and the woman who's mine now.

8

AMY

God help me, I don't know how I'm going to get Abigail and I out of this mess. I don't know how I'm going to get us away from this crazy man...

Especially now that he's calling me *his*.

Just what the hell does he mean by that? I wonder as I take a seat beside Abigail on the couch.

He called me his in the kitchen as if he thought the concept would give me comfort, but all it does is fill me with dread.

Does he intend to keep us? Like we're pets or something? Does he really think he can get away with it?

Fuck, he probably can.

Just because I slept with him once... okay, twice, doesn't mean I like the man. It was just a mistake made in the heat of the moment. A mistake I seriously don't intend on repeating—despite what just happened in the kitchen.

All I have to do is keep my distance from him. Avoid letting him touch me. Avoid touching him.

But until when?

Why, dammit?

Why does my body turn on me every time he touches me? Why, even now, do I still shiver with the memory of his kiss. Why can't his touch feel cold and disgusting like Ivan's? What makes him different?

At least I knew Ivan, I could predict him. Andrew is a complete wild card. I have no idea what he'll do next.

Abigail smiles and bounces beside me as she watches her show, and something about it just makes me want to scream in hysterical frustration. She's already adapting to this madness. The stuff that's going on is probably even starting to feel normal to her.

I've got to get her out of here.

I glance towards the front door. I'm dressed in only a t-shirt, and we don't have the necklace, or any money, or anything we could trade, but...

Fuck it, we should just make a run for it. Anything is better than staying here.

I rise to my feet and Andrew steps out of the kitchen.

My luck can't be this bad, it can't...

As if he can tell exactly what I'm thinking and he's amused by it, his lips curl up into a smirk as he regards me.

"Going somewhere, Amy?" he asks.

Out of the corner of my eye, I see Abigail tear her attention away from the TV to look up at me.

"Actually..." I drawl out just to see that smirk on his face fade away.

"Don't even think about it," he warns, taking a menacing step towards me.

Would he hurt me in front of my daughter?

I stare into his dark eyes for a long moment and come to the conclusion that yes, yes he would.

Whatever there is between us, I don't think it protects me. No, if anything, it makes my situation that much worse.

I'm no fool, I know he has all the power here.

He can do anything he wants to me, and who's to stop him? Me? Abigail?

"Amy..." he says, taking another step towards me.

Just the thought of him coming closer is enough to send me into a panic. I don't know what will happen if he gets close but I know it won't be good. And it's not because I'm afraid he'll hurt me. No, I'm afraid he'll do something worse... like kiss me again. I'd rather submit than endure that.

I'll take humiliation over the confusing attraction to keep him at a distance.

At least for now.

With a sigh, I look away and drop back down to the couch.

Andrew seems to relax, the tension going out of him. His shoulders drop and he cracks his neck.

He stares at me for a long moment, the air crackling between us, then walks over to the dining room table.

"Are you hungry?" he asks.

I shake my head. My stomach is so twisted up just the thought of food is making me feel sick.

"You should eat," he says and looks at me pointedly.

It takes me a moment to realize what he's trying to say. When I realize he's looking at my stomach, my face burns with mortification. He can't be seriously suggesting... Oh my god, he is... He's totally eluding that I could be pregnant.

I can't even.

No.

Hell no.

Oh god.

But maybe I am...

My brain just shuts down, having reached its limit of acceptable craziness.

Over the next few minutes, I'm vaguely aware of Abigail bouncing up and down beside me, singing along with a cartoon princess.

Pregnant. I could be pregnant.

In the kitchen, Andrew cleans up the mess from breakfast.

If I am, then what?

I'm so paralyzed by my thoughts, I just sit on the couch in stunned silence. I didn't think my situation could get any worse, but now it's about as bad as it could possibly get.

It's not until Andrew is done cleaning up and almost upon me that I feel like I can move again. All my muscles tense up and I'm prepared to bolt.

He drops down on the couch and wraps his arm around me just as I try to stand.

Bicep tensing, his arm squeezes around me to drag me closer to him. I try to push up. I try to scoot away from him. But my desire to move away only seems to make him that more determined.

I know this drill, we did this last night, but I can't seem to stop myself.

The more I fight him the more his hold tightens.

He traps me against his side, arm wrapping around my shoulder, and his heavy hand coming to rest on my arm.

Abigail glances over at us and he grins at her.

To my dismay, she smiles back at him.

I take a deep breath, hold it, and count to ten. If I just relax, maybe eventually his hold will loosen enough for me to escape.

I exhale the breath I was holding, and tired of staring off into space, I take a good look at him, familiarizing myself with him. After all, it's always good to know your enemy.

Last night, in the dark, I couldn't see him though I got to know him quite intimately.

In the light of day, he seems to loom even larger, if that's even possible. It must be because he's so close, practically breathing down my neck.

I look down at the huge hand upon my arm and note the scars on his knuckles. I wonder how many men he's hit with his hands. How many women? How many children?

Shivering with that thought, I jerk my gaze away only to have it fall upon his lap. I definitely don't need any reminders of how big he is in that department.

I drag my eyes up until they fall on his face.

He stares down at me with a dark, hungry intensity that takes my breath away.

Why is he looking at me like that?

And why is his big head growing even bigger?

Oh, it's because he's dipping his face, coming in for a kiss.

Leaning back, I blurt out, "If you're going to keep us stuck in this house, Abigail will need more to do. Watching cartoons all day isn't good for her."

He frowns, pausing a breath away from my lips, looking chagrinned.

"I don't know how long you intend for this to go on," I continue, now that I've got his attention. "But we'll also need some clean clothes and all our toiletries."

He nods his head, his eyes locking on my lips, and murmurs, "It's already being taken care of."

"It is?" I ask with some surprise, not expecting that answer. "In what way?" I press, more warily.

Is it being taken care of because he intends to release us? Or is it because he doesn't expect us to be alive long enough to need more than what we already have?

"Johnathan is bringing—" he starts only to be cut off by someone knocking loudly on the front door. "Speak of the devil," he mutters and unwraps his arm from around my shoulders with a look of regret.

As soon as his hold on me loosens, I pull away from him. He stands and I sink back into the couch cushions, grateful for the interruption.

Really, just sitting next to him was dangerous. I was afraid that at any moment he was going to start kissing me right in front of Abigail and I wouldn't be able to resist him.

It's not until he's halfway to the front door that I realize I'm half naked. Grabbing one of the couch pillows, I pull up my knees and hug it close, hiding my lack of pants.

"Johnathan," Andrew says coolly and steps back, giving the other man room to walk in.

Johnathan walks in and grunts before dropping the box he's carrying to the floor with a loud crash.

"Did you bring it?" Andrew asks, sounding a little impatient as Johnathan straightens and gives him a dirty look.

"Johnny!" Abigail squeals from beside me and then jumps up, running to him.

"Abigail, no!" I call out, popping up but it's too late. She's already throwing herself at the guy, hugging those tree trunks he calls legs.

"Hey, there," Johnathan grumbles and pats her on the head, looking incredibly uncomfortable.

He shoots a distressed look towards Andrew, no doubt hoping Andrew will help him, but Andrew just smirks and leans back, crossing his arms over his chest.

"Was there any trouble?" Andrew asks.

"Nothing we couldn't handle," Johnathan grumbles trying to unsuccessfully pry Abigail's little fingers off of him.

I shouldn't find it hilarious, I really shouldn't, but perhaps I've finally broken. Laughter bubbles up in my throat and I have to bite my lip to keep from releasing it.

I should probably pull Abigail off the guy, but a little, evil part of me is happy she's making him so uncomfortable. If he works with a guy like Andrew, I'm sure he deserves it.

"Well, are you just going to stand there or are you going to help me?" Johnathan asks Andrew as Abigail starts babbling about her day and how much she missed him.

Suddenly Andrew's phone starts ringing and his smirk becomes an outright wicked grin. "Sure..." he says and lifts his phone. "But first I've gotta take this."

9

ANDREW

"Andrew, my son, it's been far too long since you've come to see me."

The man on the line is trying to sound lighthearted but I hear something I can't quite place in his voice

"Father, it's been far too long since you've called me."

"That's probably true."

I motion to Johnathan to bring the boxes in without me. He's been watching me since I took the call and the finger he gives me when I start to turn away from him tells me he's not nearly as happy as I am that my phone rang.

Walking into the kitchen, I ask, "What's going on?"

"Well, I think it's high time you came back to confessional, son."

"How soon are you thinking?" I ask as I look back to

the living room where Amy is holding back Abigail from jumping all over Johnathan.

"When can you get here?" he asks.

"An hour."

"See you then, son. Don't forget your tidings though," he says before disconnecting the call.

Of course the fuck wants to hear my sins and get paid to do it.

Turning towards the group in my living room, I smile at Johnathan. "You look like crap, man. Like you haven't slept in a week."

Giving me the stink eye, he says, "You know I haven't. After this, I'm getting a bottle of tequila and drinking myself into an oblivion."

"You have such lofty ambitions for the evening, buddy."

"What do you mean *lofty*?"

"Well, I was thinking that you should hang out here for a bit. Take a load off your feet."

"What do you mean by lofty, Andrew? And I would rather... Why would I want to stay here... No. Flat out *no*."

Frowning at us both, I can see Amy isn't crazy about Johnathan staying here any more than he is.

"I gotta go to church for a bit. Father Coss needs to see my smiling face," I say to Johnathan.

"Fuck," he groans as he turns towards the door.

"Hey, language!" Amy shouts then turns to me. "What do you mean you have to leave? Church for you?!"

Nodding my head, I turn from her and head up the

stairs. I can feel her stomping up the stairs behind me, following me into our bedroom.

"You can't just leave us here with him!"

Turning my head back to her, I say, "You're just as safe with him as you are with me."

I'd rather not leave her if I didn't have to, her or Abigail. But I don't get that choice, work is work.

When Father Coss calls it's usually a good idea to go. He's like Simon in some aspects, the old man has his fingers and ears everywhere. When he calls for confession, you attend.

Walking into the bedroom closet, I start stripping off my clothes.

I pause for a moment when I hear Abigail shrieking excitedly and then Johnathan bellows, "Watch my toes, you little goblin!"

Amy looks torn between interrogating me and finding out what's happening downstairs. "Why are you leaving us with *him*? He looks like a gorilla stuffed inside a suit."

Laughing, I have to agree. "Yeah, he does."

She is about to start in on me when I shove my jeans and boxers down in one push. Her little gasp from behind me brings a grin to my lips.

Straightening back up, I turn to her. My cock is soft at the moment but her eyes are stuck there. Her cheeks turning bright red.

"Wha... Where...What are you doing?"

Feeling the hint of a rise, I flex my groin muscle at

her. My cock bobs and she rips her eyes up, staring me in the face. "What in the world are you doing?"

"Getting dressed. Like I said, I need to go to church."

"But... What does that mean?"

Pulling a pair of slacks out of a drawer, I step into one leg then the other. "I need to go talk to a man about something."

Not bothering with underwear, my cock is still dangling out as I pull on an undershirt then a dress shirt. Tucking the shirts in, Amy has to tear her eyes away from my cock again.

"Keep staring at it and I might let it bite you."

Rolling her eyes, she says, "Look, I'm not comfortable with Johnathan. I don't like any of this."

Walking past her with my socks and shoes, I say, "Look, Amy, it's only a few hours at most. Be a good girl and you'll be fine."

Those words silence her. I know she hasn't accepted her life yet. She hasn't come to the realization that things have changed so completely that she's in a completely new world. One where there are rules in place to keep her safe. But she needs to know her life is in jeopardy and by that extension so is Abigail's.

I can't allow her to do something stupid to endanger either of those.

"Amy, be a good girl. I will keep you and our little princess safe. The world outside of my door is not a safe place for you now. Until I say otherwise, you should do the smart thing and listen to me."

Her eyes are wide when I mention Abigail, her mouth opening like a fish. I don't think she caught the whole safety thing when she says, "She is not *ours,* you can't just take us like this and make us yours."

Shaking my head, I stand from the bed. I'm ready to head to the church. I don't want to leave them alone like this so soon, but life is about doing the things you don't want to do.

Striding to her, I wrap my arms around her waist before she has a chance to fight me. Leaning down, I kiss her mouth. Not gently this time, like when we were in the kitchen.

No, I kiss her like I did last night in the dark.

I'm not asking for her submission; I am taking what's mine by right. She's mine and she *will* submit.

My lips meld against hers and she fights me even now. I'm not sure if I would be so happy if she easily gave in. Thankfully, she doesn't.

Her hands come to my chest to push me away, but I keep at it. My hands pull her waist roughly to my rising cock. The hard flesh pushing against my pants and into her stomach.

It takes minutes, not moments, to get her to respond the way I want. At first, she does so tentatively, like it's her way of just getting it over with.

When I press her against the door, lifting her up, my cock pressing against her pussy and grinding hard against her, I start to feel the response I want.

Panting as I pull away from her lips, I turn my head to

the side to latch onto her neck. I'm not leaving a hickey. No, I give a quick hard bite and her squeak is all the confirmation I need to know I got what I wanted.

"Why did you bite me!?" she huffs out at me, her breath as labored as my own.

"Marking what's mine."

Setting her down, I leave her staring at me like I'm a crazy man as I leave the bedroom.

Stopping Johnathan as he unloads the last box from his SUV, I ask, "What trouble did you encounter at the apartment?"

"Five guy surveillance. Two of which will not be a problem again. They weren't the best the Russians could have used to watch her place so we didn't have any problems. Exiting was a breeze and we had no followers. It was as we thought though. They were watching and waiting for her to come back. They had their snatch and grab stuff ready to go."

Nodding my head, I say, "Alright, I'll be back in a few hours. Contact me if you need anything or should something arise. Anything else, let me know when I get back. Fucking keep an eye open though. I don't like the Russians being involved in any of this."

"You and me both, brother."

Bumping fists with me, I head to my car.

Sitting in the parking lot of Father Coss' church, I press

the number on my phone for Simon. He's the guy who is pretty much the head of intelligence for us.

"Andrew."

"Simon, got a call from Father Coss. Wants me to come in for confessional."

"Interesting. Did he give any indication of why?"

"No, but he wanted it sooner rather than later," I say.

"Understood, call me back when you're done."

Disconnecting the call, I open the door and get blasted by a gust of rain and wind. Fuck, it's going to be a chilly night.

The church I enter is one of those big old castle looking types. It's been here since Garden City was in its infancy and it hasn't really changed since. All around the church and its parking lot are modern buildings, large glass looking behemoths. But they can't top this church's imposing look.

Going through the wide double doors, I shake off the rain in the entrance. Looking out to the rows and rows of pews, I see people of all walks of life sitting or kneeling in prayer.

Father Coss is up front, speaking to a couple of elderly women. When he spots me he gives me a slight nod of his head.

Heading to the left, I go straight to the confessional booth to wait for the grizzled old man. He has the look of an old drill sergeant, not the kindly look you'd think a priest would have.

Sitting down in the booth, I lean forward to close the curtain.

I once asked Lucifer what the good father has him talk about during these 'confessional' times.

I can't forget the look he gave me when he said, "I don't go to him. He comes to speak with me."

When the old man enters the other side across the partition, I say, "Father."

"It's good to see you in church again. You haven't been around in a while. I thought you might have forgotten where it was."

"Ha!" I chuckle. He knows I wouldn't be caught dead inside of one of these boxes if it wasn't for the information he has for us.

"Laughing will only take you further from God, Andrew," he says in a tired voice.

"I'm pretty sure I've already been forgotten by the old man. No sense in getting into his bad graces now."

"Andrew, I've told you before..."

"Father, let's bypass the rhetoric." Reaching through the small panel in the back of the box, I slide the envelope full of cash his way.

"As you wish, but if you ever want to talk... Anyways, let's see what you brought me."

The ruffling of cash as he counts it makes me want to burst out laughing, but I know from experience if I do that I'll have to pay more.

Keeping my mouth shut, I wait for him to finish up.

"It makes this old priest happy to see the youth of

today taking care of the church," he says, then quietly murmurs to me. "You guys have been making some waves around the city for a while now. Any chance of you letting things die down?"

"Soon enough, I suppose, but we still have things to take care of."

"How many more bodies am I going to say last rites over before... He's satisfied?" he asks with that same tired tone.

He didn't use to always sound so tired and weary, but I think he's getting tired of living in a city like Garden City. This place will either make you or chew you up and spit you out.

"If I had that answer, Father, we wouldn't be here. He... isn't happy, and when you make him mad it's a long road to hell."

We are speaking of Lucifer of course, my boss. The man is the true power in this city, so when someone fucks with him it's a bad day for everyone.

Looking through the partition, I see Father Coss make the sign of the cross.

"There is word of something big going on, Andrew. Not on your side though. The deaths of the Yakuza have made things unstable all over the city. There was a vacuum left there and it's starting to look like the Russians are filling the void.

"What's the big thing happening?" I ask.

"That's the problem, Andrew, there aren't any whis-perings of what's happening. Just whispers of big people moving in. Tough men with dark names. The wives and mistresses of the Russians are in the dark as much as everyone else except the highest of their group. Normally, I would just pass this on to you guys and keep my peace here. But..."

He doesn't finish, and for the first time in a very long time, I feel the hairs on the back of my neck rise. I feel like I have the crosshairs of a sniper right on the back of my head. If this church wasn't made neutral by all the gangs, groups, and mafia in our city, I would be falling to the floor with my gun out, trying to make my way out of this building as fast as possible.

"Fuck," I grumble to myself.

Normally I would be reprimanded by the old priest for using such language in the house of God, but he just sighs.

"The body count for this could be very high, Andrew. I need you to get to Lucifer and the Spider. I need you to warn them and try to get them to find some way to come to peace with the city. I'm not sure we will survive the bloodshed of whatever is going to happen."

Father Coss stands up from the benches and leaves the confessional booth before I even have a chance to say anything back.

Sitting there for a moment, I try to organize my thoughts. Things are happening now outside of our scope of knowledge. Big things that could spell a shit ton of trouble for us.

Shaking my head, I stand up.

OUTSIDE, in the safety of my car, the rain starts coming down in hard waves. The wind pushes one way then the other. If the weather is matching the stirrings of the city, we might be in deep shit.

Fuck me sideways.

Dialing Simon, I try to gather my thoughts in the moments before he answers.

"Andrew, what was he wanting to talk about?"

"Shit, Simon, that's the thing. There really isn't anything to talk about beyond whispers. Whispers that have the old man terrified."

"What do you mean?" he asks.

"He's scared. Says something big is in the works on the Russian front, but he doesn't know what. Nobody is talking about it. Seems only the higher-ups know anything and they are tightlipped. Not even the mistresses are talking. One thing he said though... Said some guys are coming into the city with really bad reputations. What that means, I don't know, but it could be heavy hitters or well... anything."

There is a long silence on the phone and I can only fill it with my own. Watching the rain slash down on my windshield as the world outside goes from night to day with the crack of a lightning bolt.

"That's the reporting we have as well. Lucifer has you coming by tomorrow for dinner, I'll be there too. We'll talk more then."

"Alright. I'm going to check in with some of my contacts. See if I can find something out. Have a good night, Simon."

"You as well."

I don't immediately drive off though. My brain is running too fast right now. Little connections are struggling to be made but I can't get the picture to adjust right.

Something out there is getting ready to happen and whatever it is... it's big.

It's close to ten when I pull into the garage. The house appears to be subdued from the outside, only a couple of lights are on. When I walk in, Johnathan is sitting on the couch, watching the local news.

Amy and Abigail are nowhere to be seen.

Smelling pizza in the kitchen, I hunt down the box before I go in to see him.

"How's the old man doing?" Johnathan asks.

Shrugging my shoulders, I say, "Worried as fuck. Something's going on out there and he has no clue what it is. Whatever is going on is big, the Russians are planning something."

"Fuck me," he growls as his head falls back. "I just fucking got back from one shit storm to this."

Nodding my head, I say, "Go home and get some rest. But do me a favor, reach out to your friends around the city. See if you hear anything out of ordinary, something sounding just a bit off."

Looking at me for a moment, he says, "Will do. I'll call you tomorrow."

I finish off my slice of pizza as I hear him leaving the house. A moment later his SUV starts up.

Shutting down the lights and locking up, I head upstairs to the bedroom. Looking around the room, I see that it's missing the one person who should be there.

Walking down to Abigail's room, I look in and see Amy curled up on the bed. Walking into the room, I gently slide my arms under Amy's legs and back and lift her off the bed.

At first, she pulls herself tight into my arms, burrowing her head into my chest. It's a long moment before she looks up with wide eyes. "Wha...?"

"I'm home, baby, let's go to our bed."

10

AMY

I shouldn't feel relieved to wake up with Andrew's arms around me, but I do.

And it scares the shit out of me.

I don't want to like him, and I don't want to feel anything for him, but my body isn't giving me a choice.

This chemistry between us doesn't make any damn sense. It's completely illogical and utterly insane. I'm terrified of this man yet something is drawing me to him against my better judgment.

I wish I could just turn it off, and as he carries me into his room and lowers me to his bed, I try to do just that.

I will all my parts to feel numb. I will myself to feel nothing for him.

His hands pull away and he straightens. Looming over me in the darkness.

I shiver at the loss of his heat. At the loss of him.

Already, I'm losing this battle I'm fighting.

In the moonlight, I can see his dark eyes gleaming down at me. The way he looks at me, like he wants me, like he *owns* me, is fucking terrifying.

Immediately, I scoot away. I need some distance between us.

"I want to leave," I say, finding my voice, but even to me I sound unsure and weak. He makes me so fucking weak and a part of me hates him for that.

He shakes his head.

"I want to sleep with Abigail tonight."

"No," he says as if that's the end of it.

"But—"

"Your place is with me, in this bed."

He's crazy. How do I even argue with him?

Pressing up against the headboard of his bed, I watch him with a mixture of fear and fascination as he begins to undress.

He loosens the tie around his neck, slides it out of his collar and drops it to the floor. Slowly, as if he's in no rush, he unbuttons his shirt. His eyes never leaving me as his nimble fingers work their way down.

I have to put a stop to this. I have to find a way to make him understand... before he undoes his pants.

"Please," I beg quietly, hating myself a little for it. "Please don't do this."

Reaching the bottom button of his shirt, his fingers pause. "Do what?"

I have to look away. I have to take a deep breath

before I answer him. "What you're doing to me. It isn't right."

He's so still, for a moment I'm hopeful that I've gotten through to him. But then I look back, noticing movement.

He pushes his shirt off of his shoulders. "What am I doing to you, Amy?"

I do my best to keep my eyes locked on his face. I won't look down. I refuse to admire all the rippling muscles he was hiding under that crisp, white fabric.

I stare so long, so hard into his face, I forget to answer him.

"What am I doing to you?" he repeats, demanding an answer.

"You're confusing me," I answer him honestly.

He grins, seemingly pleased by my admission.

"I appreciate your protection," I further explain. "I really do. But you can't keep me... us..."

"I can't?" he challenges, the grin fading. He looks angry again.

My throat tightens up from the look on his face, and I shake my head.

His voice is as sharp as a bite as he asks, "Who's going to stop me?"

I struggle to answer at first. The law? No, I'm not that naïve or foolish. My family? All I have is my aunt and I don't want to get her mixed up in this. She's elderly and would probably just expect the authorities to handle it. Abigail's father? He's never given a shit.

"Who's going to stop me, Amy?" he repeats, demanding an answer.

For as long as I can remember I've been alone. It's all been on me. Paying all the bills. Being both mother and father for Abigail. I've always shouldered all the burdens and this time is no different. I have no one but myself.

Lifting my chin, I say, "I will."

Of course he finds my answer amusing. Hands hovering over his belt, he tips his head back and laughs.

Filling with righteous indignation, I stiffen against the headboard.

"I will," I repeat angrily.

Anger is good. Anger drowns out the fear. I stoke the fire. I embrace it. "You can't keep us."

"I can," he counters and quickly unbuckles his pants.

I lean my head back and squeeze my eyes shut as his pants start sliding towards the floor. Under normal circumstances, me being dressed and him being pantless would put me at an advantage... but not in this case.

The bed dips and I panic. He's going to touch me and I just know I'm going to like it. Once again my body will betray me, making me want things I shouldn't want.

"Why do you want someone who doesn't want you?" I lash out at him, hoping to push him away. "Can't you get a woman without resorting to this?"

I don't have to open my eyes to be chilled by his reaction. I can feel it. I can sense it. I can fucking taste it. But I've come too far now to go back.

I can't let him touch me. I can't let him get me pregnant.

"Do you always have to use force or—"

My ankles are grabbed and I'm yanked down the bed before I get to finish. His mouth smashes against my mouth, devouring the scream that escapes my lips.

I push at him. My hands shoving into his shoulders then pounding at his chest.

He doesn't budge an inch. If anything, my struggle only seems to spur him on, increasing the fervor of his kiss.

His tongue lashes at my tongue, attempting to whip me into submission.

I try to bring my knees up, aiming for that gigantic dick of his. Sensing the danger, he suddenly shifts. His massive legs move on top of my legs, weighing me down. Pinning me to the bed.

I feel tears of frustration stinging my eyes as the seconds tick by and my arms begin to tire from hitting him. My knuckles are bruising, and all this effort, all this violence, hasn't made a lick of difference.

His kiss begins to soften as if he's trying to soothe me. I fight him, hitting him until my arms are exhausted.

Then I just stop, giving up. Why keep fighting? He's bigger. Stronger.

Meaner.

It's all a waste of energy. Utterly useless.

His kiss deepens. His hands caress me, lulling me into compliance.

I feel drained. Empty.

Physically spent.

He shifts above me, removing some of the weight on top of my legs. His hands roam down then he pulls back just enough to pull my shirt over my head, breaking our kiss.

I stare up at him.

He looks down at me, and those dark, gleaming eyes of his soften. His hand comes back down, cupping my face.

"Why?" I ask, my voice sounding so small. Beneath him I feel so tiny.

"Don't you feel it?" he asks.

Slowly, I shake my head, lying to myself. Lying to him. I feel something, like a warmth swelling inside of my chest, but I don't know how to explain it, and certainly don't know what it is.

"It's destiny," he says huskily, his thumb dragging across my bottom lip.

"Destiny?" I repeat with a little snort of derision.

"Fate," he clarifies.

I roll my eyes up at him.

He just grins. "You can keep fighting it, Amy, but it always wins in the end."

"You're crazy," I say as his hands slide down, slipping behind me, unsnapping my bra.

"I'm not the one fighting battles I can't win."

Tensing up, I try to cross my arms to keep him from removing my bra but he just pries them apart. He slides the straps down my hands, tosses the bra to the side, then stares hungrily at breasts.

Under his gaze, my breasts begin to feel warm and heavy. My nipples tingle and tighten.

God, I hate my reaction to him.

Once more I attempt to cover myself but he just pries my arms open again.

"See," he says with some amusement. "Still fighting."

"I can't help it," I groan as his hands let go of my arms so he can fondle and caress my breasts.

"I know," he says, his fingers wrapping around me, deliciously squeezing me. "But you're only fighting yourself..."

I open my mouth to explain I'm not fighting myself, I'm fighting him, but then his mouth covers me. Sucking my nipple into his wet, hot mouth.

All thoughts go flying out of my head.

He moves side to side, cupping me, suckling on me. Worshipping each breast equally with his hands and tongue.

At first I try to ignore it. I try to shut down my senses but it just feels too damn good. Each suck, each pull, echoes in my core.

I start to squirm beneath him and grab the back of his head. I try to direct him, to show him what I want, but he won't be rushed.

He takes his time. Sucking me into his mouth. Swirling his tongue around and around then pulling back with a hard suckle.

The more and more he sucks and licks on me, the more and more I pulse and throb. I suffer it for what feels like a torturous eternity before I can take no more.

"Andrew," I groan.

I rub my legs against his legs, feeling hollow and empty.

"Mmm?" he hums, his lips vibrating against me.

I *need* to be filled.

"What are you doing?"

"Sucking on my tits," he murmurs.

"Your tits?!" I repeat incredulously and try to push up.

He pushes me back down and growls. "Yes, these are my tits and I'm enjoying them."

I shake my head, even now clenching down on emptiness. "They're not *your* breasts, they're *mine*," I moan.

He ignores me, suckling hard.

I cry out at the hard pull on my nipple and start to panic when he doesn't stop.

"Andrew," I gasp, tugging on his hair, trying to pull him off.

He just keeps sucking and sucking, until it starts to hurt. He doesn't let up until I whimper and try to shove him off.

My breast comes out of his mouth with a wet pop. His eyes roll up to stare at me as his tongue laps at me, soothing the hurt.

"These are my tits," he growls.

I open my mouth to argue with him some more but

the dark, possessive way he looks at me causes the words to stick in my throat.

"This is *my* stomach," he says, his mouth sliding down, his teeth nibbling at my skin. "These are my hips."

He grabs me hard by the hips and pushes my ass into the bed.

"This is my pussy," he purrs, shoving down my sleep pants with my panties trapped inside them.

"No," I protest, sitting up and reaching for the waistband.

"Yes," he says forcefully, pushing me back down.

He yanks hard on the pants, forcing my ass up and off the bed.

I don't know what happened, and I don't know what's caused this sudden change in him. For a few moments there, while he was sucking on my breasts, I foolishly felt safe.

I even allowed myself to want him.

But I'm not safe. I'll never be safe with this man.

As my pants reach my feet, I react instinctively, taking a little kick at him. He grabs my ankle, his grip tight, bruising.

"Amy," he says ominously. "That was a very bad idea."

I'm already fucked so I think *what the hell* and kick my other foot at him. I know it's pointless. I'm completely naked and at his mercy, but I want to hurt him.

Just a little bit.

My little kick gets him in the chest and he growls

viciously, causing all the little hairs on the back of my neck to stand on end.

Grabbing the foot that just kicked him, he roughly shoves my legs apart, spreading me wide open for him.

Desperately, I try to close my legs but I'm no match for his strength. I start to sit up and he yanks on my legs, sending me back down to the bed.

"Stop, please," I beg, sounding weak and pathetic.

He slides up and glares down at me from between my open thighs, slowly shaking his head. "I tried. God knows I tried to take it slow with you, but that's not what you want. That's not what you need, is it?"

He stares down at me and my fear begins to morph into anger again. I wrap the emotion around me like a warm, comforting blanket.

What's the worse he can do to me? My angry mind rationalizes. *Hurt me some more? Or fuck me with that big dick of his?*

"You know what I need?" I say, glaring defiantly up at him. "I need my freedom! I need my choices back!"

His fingers begin to loosen around my left leg and I seize upon the opportunity, kicking out at him.

He takes the kick to his thigh and grunts.

I try to ignore the painful tingling in my toes. I don't want to regret the kick but kicking his thigh felt like kicking a column of bricks.

He grabs my knee, shoving my legs wide open again.

"You had freedom," he sneers down at me. "And look what you did with it... You fucking squandered it."

I reel back, feeling like he just slapped me.

"You had choices," he goes on, his weight coming down on top of me. "And the choices you made brought you here. *Your* choices put you in my bed."

I take a swing at him. Wanting to slap that knowing sneer off of his face. Wanting to hurt him because his words hurt me.

This isn't my fault, it isn't, I tell myself.

But a part of me feels like it is.

My hand connects with his cheek and I don't know who's more shocked, him or me. I stare at him, my eyes widening with horror. He stares down at me, his eyes blackening with anger.

He releases his grip on my legs and I immediately flinch, expecting him to hit me back.

Instead, he grabs my hands and yanks my arms painfully up, pinning them above my head.

"I'm sorry," I groan, tears blurring my eyes as I arch my back off the bed, even now trying to yank my wrists from his grip.

"Oh, you're going to be," he snickers, and my heart lurches with fear. What's he going to do to me now? How is he going to repay me for that slap?

"Please, don't hurt me," I plead as he settles his weight on top of me.

His hard cock digs into my thigh and the weight of his stomach anchors me to the bed.

"To answer your earlier question," he says, shifting

both of my wrists into one of his hands. "I've never had to use force before..."

One hand now free, he drags it down my body and pushes it between my legs. "But there's a first time for everything."

Self-preservation kicks back in. I twist and pull on my arms as his fingers push through my folds.

"Fuck," he groans. "You're soaking wet."

Shame blooms inside of me and my face feels like it is on fire. My skin burns with my humiliation.

Even now, completely at his mercy, with the threat of him just taking what he wants hanging over my head, I want him. I fucking *ache* for him.

I'm so fucking sick.

His fingers slide through me, thick and slick with my wetness.

His head drops down and his lips push against my ear. "I'm going to force you, Amy. I'm going to force you to beg me for it," he whispers.

He leans back and looks into my eyes, savoring my reaction as his words sink in.

"I fucking hate you," I hiss, and I mean it. I so mean it. I hate him for what he's doing, but most of all I hate him because I want him.

Fat, glittering tears roll down my cheeks and he leans down again, his soft lips catching them.

"Love and hate... it's all the fucking same to me," he admits, and then his mouth smashes against mine in a soul-crushing kiss.

I taste the salt of my sadness upon his lips. I taste his desire mixing with it. His fingers continue to slide through me, circling my clit but never touching it as he kisses me.

His tongue plunges into my mouth and I consider trying to bite the fucker off.

But what will that get me? How will that help me and my situation?

Last night I gave in because it felt good and I hoped that maybe, just maybe, it would give me a little more power back. I had hoped that if I slept with him, perhaps he would be more inclined to spare me instead of killing me once they've got what they want from Ivan.

I never dreamed he didn't intend to kill me at all...

"You taste so fucking good," he groans into my mouth, and I can't stop myself from arching up.

From seeking relief from this growing, insistent throb.

His fingers circle, around and around. Gliding through my wetness. Slick with my juices.

So close but never touching me there, where I need it.

The swelling, the pulsing, it starts to drive me to distraction. I try to deepen the kiss. I try to make him forget the whole begging thing but he must sense my intention.

He breaks the kiss and starts stamping his lips down my neck. My pussy clenches down on emptiness.

"Andrew, please..." I groan, my fingers curling, my nails sinking into my palms.

"Please, what?" he breathes against my throat, his

mouth hovering over the spot he just kissed.

I press my lips together, unable to resort to begging just yet.

He chuckles and then his teeth sink into my flesh. I feel that bite resonating in the depths of my fucking soul.

"Amy," he purrs, pulling back. "All you have to do is give in and this will all be over."

I shake my head. I can't, I just can't...

But something inside of me is already breaking. My will is cracked.

He chuckles and begins to circle his fingers harder, faster.

I rock my hips up, moving in rhythm with his circles. If I could just position myself the right way, I could get his fingers exactly where I need them...

I suddenly jerk my hips up and the tips of his fingers drag across my clit.

It's just a brush, nothing more, but the sensation is so fucking wonderful. It's exactly what I crave, exactly what I need, but it's also too fleeting.

The pleasure fades quickly and somehow, I'm left even more needy. I want more. So much more...

"Amy... Amy... Amy..." he murmurs against my throat. "The only person you're hurting is yourself."

And I know deep down inside that he's right. One way or another, I'll need relief. Why should I keep torturing myself?

"Andrew..." I groan.

"Yes?" he purrs, and I can feel his cock twitch against

my thigh with anticipation.

I could just use his body to relieve myself. It doesn't mean I belong to him.

It doesn't.

"Please..." I plead, throwing my head back and thrusting my hips up. "Please..."

Put me out of my fucking misery.

"Just say it," he growls.

"Please fuck me," I beg, giving in with a sob.

His fingers move away and I almost start crying at the loss. Then his wet hand grips my hip and he's shifting himself above me.

There's no warning, no time to prepare. He drives himself inside me in one hard, powerful thrust.

"Oh god," I nearly scream.

The sensation that rolls through me is so intense it's almost too much.

"No," he grunts above me, holding himself still. I watch as his head falls forward, as he seems to struggle with himself. "Not God."

Inside me, he's so big, so thick, I'm afraid I might burst open.

"So fucking tight," he hisses, pulling his hips back, slowly sliding out of me.

I tremble beneath him.

"So fucking wet."

He drives himself back in, smashing against my clit.

"So fucking beautiful," he growls, grinding into me.

The sensation, the pleasure, it's all too much. He left

me hanging on the edge for far too long. My body locks up and my walls clamp down on his cock.

"Oh fuck," he groans as my pussy grips him, pulling him in. "Already, baby?" he croaks. "Fuck!"

I writhe against the bed, helpless, powerless, as my walls convulse around him. Milking my orgasm from him.

I'm only using him, I have to remind myself.

I fucking hate him, I repeat inside my head as I explode with bliss.

All these warm, gooey feelings... they're mine, not his.

He fights through my clench, pulling himself out and then slamming back in. Over and over again.

Fucking me like an animal.

There's no love, there's no beauty in this.

My ears ring with the sound of his skin slapping against my skin.

This is just pure, primal instinct.

His balls slap against my ass.

Two people using each other.

At least that's what I'm telling myself.

Above me, he glares down at me and beads of sweat form on his brow.

The tremors from my release begin to fade away and I have this urge to hurt him. I wish he wasn't restraining me so I could rip my nails down his back.

I want to punish him. I want to fucking damage him.

Stretching up, I do the only thing I can do. Pushing my mouth against his shoulder, I bite down, hard.

His grip around my wrists tightens and dirty, filthy words start to pour from his mouth.

I wrap my legs around his hips and lock my ankles behind his back.

He growls and snaps, pushing me down. He chest smashes against my breasts as he pounds me into the mattress.

The head of his cock bumps against the barrier of my womb and I explode.

Gushing all over him as I come again.

His roar is so loud in my ear it's deafening. And then he's growing inside of me, swelling and pulsing, but he doesn't slow.

No, he begins to fuck me harder and faster as he fills me with his sticky cum.

My body rocks up and down, and the headboard cracks against the wall.

"Amy," he roars my name, and for a moment I'm weak. I feel myself starting to let him in.

But then his thrusts begin to slow and his breath is hot against my ear as he says, "You're mine."

I try to jerk away. I turn my face to the side but I can't escape his lips.

"You're mine now. You belong to me," he grunts into my ear as his hips roll deep, grinding into my clit.

I whimper and writhe beneath him, too sensitive after all my orgasms.

"And if I'm not fucking mistaken," he sighs, finally stilling above me. "I just got you pregnant."

A my's hasn't stopped glaring at me since this morning. Thinking about it though, it might have started last night when she tried to pull away from me after I got her pregnant.

I don't think she could have tried any harder to get away from me after I told her. She squirmed and raged at me, hitting me and kicking me with all her small might. I'm a big man, though, and there was only so much she could do with her fists.

After she finally wore herself out, I pulled her tight to my chest. Holding her in my arms last night, listening to her slow, even breathing gave me the time to get my thoughts in order.

First thing; I have a child on the way. I'm certain of it. I feel it in the very marrow of my bones.

After I poured myself into her, I felt a spark of life. Our lives will forever be entwined now.

Marrying Amy should be a top priority. The paperwork won't be a problem but the vows should be interesting. If she fights as hard about the vows as she did with my claiming her, I might have to do the same thing right then and there on the alter. That could cause some issues with the priests... but nothing money wouldn't fix.

Second thing is I need to get my house in order. The one we're in now isn't what I think of when I see my family in my head. Amy, Abigail, and our soon-to-be-born. We need a bigger house, and maybe a housekeeper/nanny to help Amy out.

Abigail is mine, I meant it when I said that to Amy. I need to get her back into a regular routine so she can adjust to this as quickly as possible. Having Abigail on my side of things will make the transition easier for Amy in the long run.

Everything comes back to Amy though. She is my reason for being now.

She fights like a little hellcat when I force her to do what's best. I like it though. She's a fighter, and she doesn't just give in to what others want.

Did I hit the nail on the head when I told her that her choices brought her to this point and time? I'm pretty sure I did. She needs to know her choices determine her fate. And she needs to know her fate is now entwined with mine.

Forever.

Peering into the rearview mirror, I smile at Abigail as she sings quietly to herself, watching the world beyond her window passing by. She's going to make a great ally. This morning, after breakfast, I called her Princess again. She likes that, and she likes it when I praise her for her good manners at the table.

It amazes me how adaptable children can be. They don't have a lifetime of fears and frustrations behind them. Amy has those fears, those frustrations of never being who she truly needs to be. She can do that now; she just needs to break through the wall that she has built up.

There are more guards around the compound than usual when I pull up to the gates, and they're all outfitted with full tactical gear and automatic rifles.

Something way out of the norm is going on.

Amy's eyes widen with fright and she reaches over to grab my hand. "Where are you taking us?"

"I've already told you, Lucifer's for dinner."

That she is grabbing my hand for support in her fear is a sign of just how worried she is. She may be pissed at me, but she knows I am her guardian angel.

"You're safe, Amy, I promise you," I say in a quiet murmur.

"But... why is everyone armed? It looks like we're entering a bunker or something."

"This is Lucifer's home; his wife and children live here. He has to have this protection. Something's up though, it isn't usually this tense."

Rolling down my window at the gate, I nod to Thad. "What's going on?"

"Lucifer has pulled almost everyone in. He's even brought in a ton of extra security. Don't know why though, but he has us on high alert. Shoot to kill orders throughout."

Nodding my head, I pull through the gate and drive into the compound. The house is fucking huge here, along with the unattached garage and servant's living quarters. This place is more like a small palace. I don't think I want my girls and child living in a place this big, but we need something more than the rinky-dink house we are currently in.

Why the fuck are we on high alert though? And why the fuck was I not notified of it is beyond me.... Fuck.

Shit is going from bad to worse with the war going on outside these walls. My body gets that tingly feeling again. Something is starting to majorly suck.

Getting out of the car, I walk to the front passenger door and then the back door. I drilled both of my girls on this. Amy was aggravated I was taking away even allowing her to open her own door from her. Abigail feels more like a princess because of it.

Neither really have a choice, they are mine to protect.

Fuck, I need to think about updating my car. I need something more bulletproof, like the Rolls-Royce Lucifer has his family driven in. Maybe a BMW or Mercedes.

It's still cold out today. I was hoping it would warm up but if anything, the temperature has dropped. Amy shivers beside me, but I don't think it's because of the temperature.

After helping Abigail out of the car, I kneel down in front of her. "Princess, I need you to promise me something."

Nodding her head eagerly, she says, "Sure!"

"Can you be on your best behavior? I need you to show everyone how good your manners are."

"Promise I will. Is Johnny going to be here?"

Nodding my head, I grin, "Yep, and you can torture him all you want."

"Goody."

W ALKING in through the front door, I smile to Lily and Lucifer. Amy's hand is crushing mine in a death grip as I pull her gently forward to introduce her to the family.

"Sir, ma'am, this is Amy and our little princess Abigail."

Smiling warmly to us both, Lucifer says, "Thank you for coming to our home for dinner. Let me introduce my family. This is Lily, Adam, and our little Evie."

Small talk and pleasantries aren't something I've done much of, but Abigail pulls our little trio out of our shells quickly. Rushing over to where Adam and Evie stand, she starts jabbering a mile a minute to Evie. She looks over at Adam only briefly, but I catch the smile she gives him.

Lily comes to Amy, taking her arm in hers. "It is *sooo*

good to meet you! I was afraid all of Matthew's men were the type who didn't have families!"

Amy turns her head to me, looking confused. "Matthew?"

Laughing quietly, Lily pulls her down the hall towards the living room, following the children. "Oh, you know, it's *Lucifer's* real name."

Lucifer eyes his wife's back, but I don't see any malice in it. If I'm not mistaken, he appears to be amused by what she said.

Once the girls are gone, he looks to Adam, who has remained behind to watch his father. They don't speak but I swear that there's a conversation going on between them.

Nodding his head to his father, Adam says, "I'm going to keep track of the girls. Make sure they don't get into any trouble."

Turning away from us, the boy walks through the house like he's the king here.

Lucifer looks proud at his son. That shit fucking disappears though as soon as he turns back to me.

His eyes go cold and his smile turns to a razor grimace.

He's not happy. Fuck.

Motioning me towards the staircase, he says, "Simon's already here, we need to talk."

Nodding my head, I follow him up the stairs. I'm not as worried as I could be right now since I'm following.

If he was following me, I would be shitting myself.

This house isn't just a compound as much as it is a fortress. If he followed me somewhere it would be because he's pushing me to my final destination. He hasn't done anything of note since he brought his family here... but I never put anything past Lucifer.

Especially if he wants something done.

This end of the house is eerily quiet as we make our way to his office. Walking into the room, Simon is already seated at the desk, looking through a thick printout of information.

"Simon, I take it me being pulled in isn't just a social call?"

"No, although I know Lily was supremely happy that we were having guests," Lucifer answers.

Sitting myself down beside Simon, I say, "Good, I think it will do Amy good to see how her life will be changing."

Simon and Lucifer exchange looks. I feel my stomach drop. Little goosebumps breakout up and down my arms. The hair on my neck is starting to stand up.

Shifting to place the weight of my body on my left side, I move my arm just a fraction. I have my gun on my right hip, it's clip is full of hollow point bullets.

Simon turns towards me and I know he won't be my first target.

No, the devil himself has to die first.

"Ivan knew far more than we thought he would, Andrew. Much of what you told me last night from the priest matches up to the info we got from Ivan."

Nodding my head, I keep my eyes trained on Lucifer. I can listen and prepare for battle if I need to. "So he knows about the guys the mafia is pulling into the city then?"

Lucifer takes over and he stares right back at me. "Yes, enough that we now have our guys watching them closely."

Simon says, "They were planning on attacking the school where Adam attends, as well as the preschool that Evie goes to."

This is not the news I was expecting to hear. I keep my body loose as I turn my eyes to Simon. "Are you fucking with me?"

"Do I have a sense of humor, Andrew?" Simon snaps at me.

He's fully aware of the tension in the room. I can see he knows more about the talk we are having and he's got more information to tell me.

"When's the hit supposed to happen?" I ask as I look back at Lucifer.

I don't like being on edge right now. I don't like the thoughts that race through my mind of what could be happening with the guys being brought in. The Russians never do anything in half measures. Shit like this is as serious as could be.

"Two days from now."

"So we hit them tomorrow," I say.

Something's not lining up right now though. What was the look for after I mentioned my girls? They aren't a part of the hit. No, something else is happening...

"Agreed. I want you and your detail to take the squad that would be heading to Evelyn's school out. Johnathan and his men will take the other squad."

"Okay," I say, "What about the Russians?"

"We have something planned for them. We will be sending a message of our own," Simon says. "Today, we've been making a lot of connections with them to the Yakuza. Connections we weren't seeing before."

"What about our boy, Ivan? What was his part?"

Lucifer frowns. "He was financing the guys coming in and the land grab that's being planned against us."

"That's it? I don't buy it."

"Neither do we, but it's what we have right now, and what he could give us," Simon tells me.

"So, what did you do with him?" I ask.

"We'll be releasing him Thursday," Lucifer says as he eyes me.

That's the shoe that was about to drop. They are letting my Amy's would-be stalker free. They are letting that waste of fucking flesh live.

"Why?" I ask through clenched teeth.

"We have a noose around his neck. We want to see where it leads," Lucifer says.

"Fine, but I don't trust that snake. He's not the forgiving type."

"That's what we wanted to talk to you about," Simon says. "He's demanded Amy be returned to him."

"*No.*"

My body has fully shifted now. I'm not a traitor to my

boss, but I will never let my girls and unborn child go. Not while I breathe.

Fuck, even if I'm dead that motherfucker will not touch them. I'll burn down hell itself to get back to them.

Simon may be a deadly man with his information, hell, he's a pretty good killer too, but Lucifer will come for me first. It will be him, not Simon. There aren't any footsteps outside the door, that's not Lucifer's way.

He'll kill his soldier himself or at least try to.

Not a word is said for three full minutes.

Nobody moves.

No sound comes from us. I'm seconds away from releasing hell on this room. I don't see this as betrayal, no this is me protecting what's *mine*.

In this life we take what's ours, we fight for what's ours, and we kill those who try to take it from us.

As suddenly as the silence starts, Lucifer cracks a smile and I hear Simon grumble out, "Fucking nuts, the both of you."

I don't relax, I'm going to kill someone. Killing someone should never be done while laughing.

Shaking his head, Lucifer says, "You owe me, Simon. Pay up."

"I should have known better," Simon says as he pulls an envelope stuffed full of cash out of his suit pocket.

Lucifer opens a drawer on the right side of the desk and my hand goes to my gun.

"Calm yourself, Andrew. Amy isn't going anywhere but home with you."

Accepting the envelope from Simon, Lucifer slides it in the desk.

Simon stands up, grumbling as he says, "Andrew, you just cost me five thousand dollars because of your caveman and his woman shit."

Shaking his head, he says before leaving the room, "I'll report back in tomorrow, Matthew. I'm going to go through all the information again, to see if I missed anything."

My hand is close to my gun, just the tips of my fingers resting on the handle. "What was the wager?"

Smirking, Lucifer says, "I bet Simon that you would rather put your future with your gun than let her go. He said not all men are captivated by a woman like I was with Lily."

Moving my hand back to my lap, I say, "Ivan needs to die."

"I agree, but right now we need to see where our little rat leads us."

"What did he say about Amy?" I ask.

"He demanded we turn her over."

"Not happening. Shit, for fun we should tell that wife of his about him having a mistress. She's the one who's worth all that money, isn't she?"

"It's a good idea, and once tomorrow is over we just might."

We stand from the desk a few minutes later and head down to the women and children.

He stops me just as we step off the stairs.

Placing a hand on my shoulder, he turns me to face him. "Don't ever put my fucking faith in you to the test, Andrew. One of us would not leave the room."

Smiling, I say, "I'm your man, Lucifer. But don't ever think of my girls or unborn child as anyone's but mine."

Raising an eyebrow, he nods his head. "Andrew, congratulations are in order then. Will there be a wedding soon?"

"I have to tame her first."

"Please, call me Lily," Lucifer's wife smiles at me once we're settled on the couch in her luxurious living room. "Only Matthew calls me Lilith."

This house is huge, like a palace or a museum, and every room we've passed through so far is elegantly appointed. I'd be in awe if I wasn't so on edge.

Obviously being evil pays well.

I return Lily's smile, trying to relax a little, but it's hard to feel comfortable in the home of the devil. Just knowing I'm in his private domain is about to give me a panic attack.

"Wine?" she asks, and I quickly nod my head.

A little booze might be exactly what I need to relax.

She leans forward and begins to pour two glasses.

I glance towards Abigail, checking on her. Unlike me,

she seems to be enjoying herself. She and Evie have already declared that they're best friends.

The children have settled on a carpet in front of the roaring fireplace. Evie and Abigail babble and giggle non-stop, playing happily with a pile of dolls and dresses, but Adam holds himself away, just watching them. For a boy so young he looks entirely too stiff and serious.

Well, I suppose if Lucifer was my father I'd be very serious too.

Lily straightens from the table and hands me a full glass.

"To new friendships," she smiles, lifting her glass in cheers.

"To new friendships," I croak and lift my glass. My smile is so tight I'm afraid my lips might split.

She nods with approval and tips her glass back. I start to lift my glass to my lips and then suddenly remember I could be pregnant...

Shit.

"What's wrong?" Lily asks, lowering her glass and frowning at me with concern.

Lowering my glass, I stare down at the deep, red liquid. How can I even explain it? Does she have any clue what her husband does behind her back? I seriously doubt it.

"I... I..." I can't even get the words past my lips so I just give up and shake my head.

"Is it the wine? I'm sorry. I'm not at all knowledgeable

when it comes to picking it. I just grabbed a bottle from Matthew's private cellar and assumed it was good."

I glance up from my glass and Lily looks so upset that I feel the strongest urge to reassure her that it's not the wine. "No, I'm sorry, it's not the wine. I'm sure the wine is very good."

Lily smiles, looking relieved for a moment but then she's frowning again. "Is it something I've done?"

"No," I say quickly. "You've been a very gracious hostess..."

Lily nods her head slowly and leans back. She doesn't seem offended by my refusal to drink the wine, if anything she seems to be simply curious now.

She regards me over the rim of her glass for a long moment before she takes another sip.

I glance towards the door, hoping that someone will appear to save me from this situation. Lily seems so nice, I don't know how to interact with her. A part of me assumed she would be mean or stuck-up given how flawlessly beautiful she is. Or as cruel as her husband. But she's practically tripping over herself to make me comfortable.

"Matthew did something, didn't he?" she finally says knowingly.

I immediately stiffen in reaction. Shit, shit, shit. I want to deny it but I just can't.

Leaving me alone with her was a bad idea. What was Lucifer and Andrew thinking? I'm not at all good at deceiving others. I hate lying, and I really suck at it.

Her eyes narrow, and the way she looks at me I get the impression that she's starting to figure it out on her own. "You know, I've been with Matthew for a little over a year now and you're the first wife I've ever been introduced to..."

"Andrew and I are not married," I quietly correct her. I have to set my glass of wine down on the table before I give in to the urge to drink deeply from it. "I've only known him for two days."

"You're kidding," she exclaims shrilly and then blushes, casting a quick look towards the children.

Adam glances over, looking at his mom curiously, but Evie and Abigail are in their own happy little world, completely oblivious of us.

"I'm not kidding, though I wish I was," I say, shifting uncomfortably.

I feel like I've already said too much and I'm afraid of what will happen if Lucifer and Andrew were to get wind of this. I wasn't specifically told not to talk or reveal why I'm with Andrew, but I just figured that it was something understood.

Not to mention I have no clue what Lily will do if I tell her the truth. Would she even believe me if I told her? If I were in her situation, I probably wouldn't.

Lily leans towards me and drops her voice to a whisper. "He took you, didn't he?"

I'm so surprised she guessed it right, I blurt out, "Yes!"

I slap a hand over my mouth and look worriedly

towards Abigail. She glances over at me, smiles sweetly, and then goes right back to playing.

My heart pounds frantically behind my ribs and my mind races a mile a minute. How much does Lily know? Does she already know everything and this is some kind of test?

Or is she someone who could help me get out of this situation?

I lean towards Lily and lower my voice to a whisper. "How did you know?"

Her eyes light up with something. Joy? Or is it amusement?

She looks almost as eager as I feel, like she too has been dying to say something.

As she sets her glass down on the table and turns back to give me her full attention, I feel this strange jolt, like we're kindred spirits in this moment.

Her lips curve into a mischievous grin and she leans in close as she whispers. "Because Matthew took me... from my husband."

Lily proceeds to tell me a whispered story about Lucifer appearing in her bedroom one night and strong-arming her and her children away from her husband. Apparently, her husband at the time, Marshall, was an awful man. He cared nothing for her or the children, and she was planning on divorcing him.

But then Lucifer swept into her life, claimed her and the children as his own, and changed all of her plans. Some of the details are fuzzy. She kind of brushes over

Marshall kidnapping her and Lucifer taking care of him, but doesn't provide any specific details.

"Are you happy?" I ask her, letting it all sink in my brain.

The story is so dramatic, so crazy, I wouldn't believe it if I didn't go through something similar myself.

She doesn't hesitate. Her lips curve into a smile and she nods her head. "Incredibly."

"Wow," I murmur and shake my head. I almost can't believe it.

Her smile sharpens and her eyes sparkle at me over the rim of her wine glass. "I told you mine, now it's your turn to tell me yours. I want all the dirty little details, and I mean *all* of them."

I hesitate, feeling suddenly self-conscious.

"Come on," Lily prods me. "Don't be a tease."

I smirk and shake my head. "I don't even know where to begin..."

Lily rolls her eyes. "At the beginning, of course."

Unlike her, my story doesn't start with Andrew, it starts with Ivan.

After taking a deep breath and figuring out where to begin, I tell her how Ivan and I met. How lucky I felt until he started getting pissed off because I wasn't ready to sleep with him until I got to know him. How quickly the situation escalated.

The stalking and the surveillance.

The pressure and manipulation.

"What a dickhead," Lily hisses after I tell her how

Ivan got me fired from the boutique I worked at just because I used work as an excuse not to see him.

I nod my head, fully agreeing with her, but that wasn't the worse of it. The worse was the beatings. All the times he'd hit me in anger when I fought him... But I don't bring those up. I don't know why, but I just can't.

Instead, I recount how I couldn't find work and how I was living off of my savings.

"He was probably telling them not to hire you," she growls.

I nod my head. "I pretty much figured that." After the twentieth rejection or so.

With a snort, she tosses the rest of her wine back, and I fight back a smile, flattered that she is so annoyed on my behalf.

"Then what happened?" she asks while leaning forward and setting her empty glass down on the table.

My amusement fades as I remember and recount the events of two nights ago. Just like she glossed over the details of Lucifer taking care of her former husband, I purposely omit Lucifer holding a gun to my head. I'm not sure how she would react to that bit of information, and I'm starting to like her too much to risk our newly minted friendship.

Not to mention I don't want to do or say anything that would piss that man off. I like my head right where it is, thank you.

"I'm glad Andrew is keeping you," she says when I finish.

I nod my head but I can't quite bring myself to verbally agree with her.

"You're not, though?" she asks.

Like I said earlier, I really suck at lying. I could try to pretend I'm happy with the situation but even a blind man could probably see that I'm not.

"Honestly?" I ask.

She nods her head.

"No," I drawl out. "I'm not happy with the situation. I'd prefer my freedom."

She scowls at me. "But Andrew will take care of you."

"Yes, but he's a stranger," I explain. "I hardly know the man. He could be just as bad as Ivan..."

Lily shakes her head vehemently. "He is nothing like Ivan. That man is scum and Andrew is one of my husband's most trusted men. He's a step above the rest."

"Perhaps you're right," I concede because I honestly don't know enough about Andrew to argue with her regarding the state of his character. What I do know, however, is that just like Ivan, he's manipulating me into a situation I don't want to be in. "He's holding me prisoner in his house."

Again, she's quick to come to his defense. "I'm sure in time, when he can trust you, he'll give you more freedom."

I shake my head in dismay. "You know this from experience?"

She sharply nods her head. "Yes."

I sigh and take a second to really think my words over

before I say them. "I know things worked out for you and Lucifer, but Andrew and Lucifer are two very different men."

I don't point out how different she and I are, and our respective situations, but I can feel it hanging in the air between us.

"I agree," she concedes. "Matthew and Andrew are two very different men, but they share the same philosophies and fundamental beliefs. They look at the world in a very..."

She trails off, her brows furrowing together in thought. "There is a word for it but at the moment it is eluding me. The way they look at the world is..."

"Radical?" I offer.

She snorts and narrows her eyes at me, obviously not finding my suggestion funny. "I was thinking more along the lines of *unique*."

I smirk at her and say, "Radically unique."

She rolls her eyes but she's smiling. "Very well, the way they look at the world is radically unique."

She looks at me, waiting for me to agree or disagree. I incline my head and she smiles, going on. "Before I met Matthew, I was blind. But he opened up my eyes and now I see the world for what it really is. Before him I was just another one of the sheep..."

"Sheep?" I repeat. "What do you mean?"

She sighs and brushes some invisible hair out of her face, looking a little flustered. "How to put this? Matthew is so much better at explaining this..." She glances over at the children and lowers her voice, as if she's suddenly worried about them overhearing. "These men, they are fierce and they are powerful, and they see the world for what it really is. They see through all the bullshit."

"Okay..." I drawl out, kind of getting it, but not really getting it. "But what makes someone a sheep?"

"A sheep is a person who believes the laws and rules are there to protect them. To make the playing field more fair when they're really there to—"

"Excuse me, Lily?"

We both turn in surprise. A middle-aged woman stands in the doorway, cradling a little bundle in her arms.

"Yes, Mary?" Lily smiles at the woman, not looking the least bit irritated by the interruption. In fact, she looks rather relieved.

"Little David is ready for bed. I thought you'd like to say goodnight before I lay him down."

"Of course," Lily beams at the woman and holds out her arms.

Mary returns Lily's smile and approaches, carefully handling the little bundle over. Once the bundle is safely in Lily's arms, Mary takes a step back and glances over at me. I smile politely at her and then we both turn our attention to Lily.

Lily smiles and nudges some of the blanket out of the way, revealing a tiny golden head.

She coos and speaks sweetly to her baby, and

watching her, I experience the strangest pang. Like there's a spot inside of me that I didn't realize was empty.

"I didn't know you had a baby," I say softly.

Lily glances up at me and gently nods her head. "His name is David."

"How old is he?" I ask, scooting a little closer to get a better look.

"Three months," she answers with a proud smile. "Would you like to hold him?"

"Yes," I fairly gush. I haven't held a baby since Abigail was born and I suddenly miss it.

Lily scoots closer to me and I extend my arms, ready to accept him. Carefully, Lily places him in my arms.

"He's fallen asleep," she whispers.

I look down at the sleeping baby in my arms and the sight of his beautiful little face steals all the breath from my lungs.

I'm stunned speechless.

Beside me, Lily chuckles quietly. "He tends to have that effect on people."

I shake my head, trying to clear it, but I still can't seem to take my eyes off of him.

"He's perfect..." I choke out, marveling at his angelic features. He's the most beautiful thing I've ever laid eyes on.

"He is," an amused male voice agrees from the doorway.

I finally manage to tear my eyes away from David's

beautiful face and glance up to see the grown-up version of him smirking down at me.

I don't know why but I feel like I've just been caught doing something I wasn't supposed to be doing.

"Thank you for letting me hold him," I say softly to Lily.

She nods and smiles as I gently hand David back to her.

Lucifer strides into the room and walks up to the couch. Bending over the back of it, he places a quick kiss on Lily's cheek and then peers down at his son.

"Mary was just about to put him in his bed," Lily murmurs quietly and leans into Lucifer.

He smiles and reaches down to stroke his son's head.

As they lean into each other, staring down at their sleeping child, the moment is so sweet, so tender, my chest tightens and I ache with a confusing jealousy.

It takes me a second to realize I want what they have.

I want the love, and I want the tenderness.

Once the realization sinks in, I abruptly turn away, feeling like an intruder peeping in on a private moment.

Lucifer straightens away first and then Lily reluctantly hands David off to Mary.

"Sweet dreams, little one," she murmurs sweetly as Mary wraps him back up and carries him out of the room.

"Shall we head into dinner?" Lucifer asks once Mary is gone, and I finally notice the dark shadow lurking in the doorway.

How long has he been standing there? Has he been there the whole time?

Andrew's eyes bore into me, burning with a dark intensity. "I'm starving," he grins.

And I've suddenly lost my appetite.

13

AMY

Dinner is a torturous affair for me, though everyone else seems to be enjoying themselves. Lily tries hard to keep me engaged in the conversation going on around the table but between having Lucifer seated across from me and Andrew directly beside me, it takes all my concentration just to get food down my throat.

And I have to eat, everyone pretty much expects it from me now. Andrew dropped the bomb and told everyone I'm expecting.

I don't know what the hell is wrong with him.

I know he wants me to be pregnant, but it's way too damn early to tell. I keep telling myself that he's going to be pretty fucking embarrassed when it turns out that I'm not pregnant. But I have this stupid feeling that he's not going to be embarrassed at all. That he's a man used to getting what he wants, and his will alone is powerful enough to knock me up.

I know, I know, now I'm the one who's thinking crazy. But this entire situation is fucking with me. Everyone around me is so happy, gathered around the table like it's one great big happy family.

And I feel like I'm the odd man out.

I'm surrounded by murderers, kidnappers, and adulterers, and yet I wonder if I should be trying harder to fit in.

When I really think about it though, especially when they're all so polite and considerate of me, I have to wonder who am I to judge?

I don't know for certain that Lucifer, Andrew, or any of the other men sitting at this table are murderers.

It's just a gut feeling I have.

Sure they grabbed Ivan and I, but I'm still alive, aren't I?

And it's not like I'm exactly free from sin. Lord knows I've made my own mistakes.

Lots and lots of them.

"Our princess looks tired," Andrew murmurs beside me, and that word, *our*, strikes a nerve in me.

I can understand why he wants to claim me, so he can use me for my body, but I don't understand why he's claiming her... unless he's serious about us being his.

I look towards Abigail and she is indeed nodding off in her chair with her spoon hanging precariously above her bowl.

"You look tired as well," he murmurs, gently grabbing me by the chin and turning my face towards him. "Are you ready to go home?"

I peer into his dark eyes, searching for the evil staining his soul, but all I see is warmth and concern.

His thumb strokes against my cheek and his touch is so warm, so nice, my skin prickles with goosebumps.

"Yes," I answer, my voice weak and barely above a whisper.

His lips curve into a smile and damn if that smile doesn't give me butterflies.

Butterflies that flutter towards my core.

I look away, wishing I knew how to destroy the power he holds over me. Inside my mind, I can hate and hate and hate, but when he touches me all that hate goes flying out the window.

Andrew grabs my hand and we stand. We say our goodbyes and Lily makes me promise to pay her a visit during the week. After having a word with Lucifer, Andrew picks up Abigail and we head to the car.

Abigail doesn't stir at all. She's so tired she curls into Andrew, clinging to him as he gets her buckled in, and then she's softly snoring by the time we pull out.

The drive is quiet, almost peaceful. I stare out the window, into the night. The lights of the city streak by, white, yellow, blue and red.

It feels good just to be outside, to be exposed to possibilities again.

Beside me, Andrew is silent and radiating tension. I

look towards him and for a split second our eyes meet. The strongest jolt courses through me like I've been struck by lightning.

There are so many words between us, hanging in the air, unspoken.

To speak them, though, would be to acknowledge them, and right now I just can't do it.

I don't know what I'm feeling anymore. I don't know how I feel about *him*.

Is his baby really growing inside me? I place a hand on my tummy and turn back to the window.

Everything is changing—my life, the way I think...

My body.

I could have what Lily has, if I allowed myself to want it...

Am I going insane?

Our situations are completely different.

I glance back at Andrew. As if he was expecting my attention, he reaches over and strokes my cheek.

Damn him. Why did he have to do that? Why does he have to be *nice* to me? Why can't he just be an asshole like Ivan?

I jerk away and twist in my seat, turning my entire body away from him.

Am I seriously getting angry because he's being nice to me? Now I know I've truly gone off the deep end.

His hand comes down on my thigh.

Warm, heavy, and possessive.

His fingers curl around me and squeeze.

I look to him again and glare, using my eyes to tell him to stop touching me. To stop breaking me down with his affection.

He smirks and his hand begins to slide up, towards the hem of my skirt. I will myself to be disgusted by his touch, to be unaffected as his skin slides against my skin, but I'm only human.

God help me, I'm not strong enough to resist this man. He's everything I could ever want, strong, protective, and affectionate. When he touches me, I come alive. And when he stops touching me, it feels like I'm dying a slow death.

I'm fighting a losing battle. Maybe it's time to admit that. Maybe it's time to just give up and give in.

To see where this craziness takes us.

We pull up to the house he called *home* and his hand leaves my thigh. I almost grab his hand to retain my connection to him.

The suggestion, *maybe we could drive around for just a little longer*, is poised on my lips but I don't let it pass.

Abigail is exhausted and needs her bed.

He gets out of the car and comes around to open my door. He helps me out and then takes care of Abigail, picking her up and carrying her into the house.

I follow behind him, shutting all the doors behind us and locking them.

The irony is not lost on me.

Up the stairs, I follow behind him.

The way he cradles and carries Abigail, it's like he's carrying the most precious package in the world.

We enter her room.

Gently, he lays Abigail down on her bed and draws up the covers, tucking her in. Stepping back, he gives me just enough room to squeeze in. I bend over her, stroke her hair back and give her a kiss goodnight on her forehead.

She smiles in her sleep.

As long as she is safe and happy, I can endure anything.

Even this man.

Straightening away, I turn to find Andrew holding out his hand.

I hesitate, looking up at his face and all the dark tenderness there before I place my hand in his. His fingers curl around mine and even this innocent touch is enough to quicken my breath.

Instead of becoming desensitized to him over time, I seem to be becoming more and more responsive to him.

He leads me out of Abigail's room and down the hall to his... no, our room.

With each step, my heart beats a little faster. And with each step, I sense a change coming over him. His grip on my hand tightens with tension and his face hardens with determination.

Have I done something to anger him? I wonder. I'm not sure but something certainly has.

He pulls me into the room and quickly shuts the door behind us.

Locking it.

I glance up at him in surprise. Something is very wrong. He was so calm, so affectionate a few moments ago... but maybe that was just the calm before the storm? Right now he looks like he's about ready to unleash on me.

"We need to talk," he says gruffly and drops my hand.

He reaches up, tugs on the knot of his tie and then yanks it out of his collar.

"What about?" I gulp and take a step back.

The drive home was so quiet, I almost forgot to be frightened of him.

Tie gone, he starts unbuttoning his shirt, his movements sharp and quick.

"About Ivan," he growls.

"What about him?" I ask, and nervously lick my lips. My mouth is suddenly dry and my stomach twists with apprehension.

He rips his shirt off and then cracks his neck.

Head straightening, he stares at me for several long, tense seconds before saying, "We're releasing him."

Fuck. My worst nightmare is coming true.

"When?" I ask, trying to come to terms with the information.

"Tomorrow," Andrew says, his eyes never leaving me. He stares at me long and hard, taking in my reaction.

"Why didn't you..." I stop and swallow. I can't even finish my question.

Perhaps it makes me just as bad as him, but a sick,

twisted part of me was hoping that Lucifer would find a reason to take care of Ivan once they got the information they wanted out of him.

I was hoping I'd never have to see him again. I'd never have to fear him again.

Andrew sneers. "Why didn't we kill him?"

Slowly, I nod my head.

"Because we still have a use for him."

My heart lurches and my breathing quickens. I have to swallow again as bile creeps up my throat. Of course they have a use for him. Ivan is no doubt a never-ending fountain of information.

But he'll want me back.

"Oh god," I groan.

I waver on my feet then I tip my head back and peer up into Andrew's hard, unforgiving eyes. "You have to let me go."

His eyes blacken and the word is nearly a roar when it comes out of his mouth. "No."

I should be afraid of Andrew's reaction and his furious expression, but right now I'm much more afraid of Ivan.

"But he's going to look for me," I begin to tearfully explain. My panic ratchets up with each word I speak, knowing deep down in my soul that they're true. "He always finds me. *Always*."

"I'll fucking kill him if he tries to take you from me."

I shake my head, wanting to believe him but knowing it's not as simple as that. Ivan has uncanny luck and very deep pockets. Eventually, he'll find me. If not tomorrow, then the day after that. And then...

"What? You don't believe me?" Andrew asks, his voice softer but somehow more dangerous.

He takes a step toward me, filling up the space I created between us. His hand reaches down, his touch tender and soft at first but then he grips my chin and yanks it up. "I almost drew on Lucifer when I learned Ivan asked for you back."

My eyes widen and my lungs freeze behind my ribs. Try as I might I can't seem to draw air into them.

"I want to rip Ivan apart with my bare hands. I want to tear him limb from fucking limb and piss all over his rotting carcass for daring to ask for you back."

Scraping up the last bits of my courage, I finally draw in some air and then ask the one question I've been dreading.

"Are you going to give me back?" I stammer out.

He might not have a choice, Lucifer might force the issue.

"No!" Andrew roars and pulls me into his chest. His grip on my chin is so hard it's almost bruising. "What part of *you're mine* is so fucking hard to understand? I'm never fucking giving you back."

In this case, the devil I know is scarier than Andrew. After all, Andrew hasn't actually hurt me, yet.

"But," I argue. "You've only known me for a couple of days. You don't know if you'll want me around forever."

Andrew just stares at me, his expression darkening.

The longer he stares at me, the more I feel like I've just made a huge mistake.

I try to pull away, try to free myself from his grip but he pulls me back.

His bare chest rises and falls, and his black eyes flash with menace. "I see you haven't accepted your fate yet."

Before I can ask him what my fate is, he lifts me up, off my feet, and carries me over to the bed.

"I thought I made this very clear," he says, and proceeds to dump me onto the mattress. "But if you need a demonstration, I'll give you a fucking demonstration."

My hair in my face, I sit up and try to brush it out of my eyes, but then my blouse is grabbed and yanked violently over my head.

"Andrew," I squeak and just manage to get the hair out of my face before he's pushing me back. He grabs the waist of my skirt and rips it down my legs.

I hear threads popping and fabric tearing.

"What are you doing?"

The only answer I get is an angry growl.

Warm hands slide under me, cupping my ass, and then they yank my panties down.

"I'm sorry," I say, hoping to quickly appease him, though I'm not sure how I pissed him off in the first place.

His hands grab my knees and then my legs are spread apart.

I look down, staring at him as he undoes his pants. The sound of his zipper being ripped down is as loud as a gunshot.

Why was I afraid of Ivan again? I wonder, staring at Andrew. It's hard to remember with him between my legs, a tower of powerful, rippling muscle.

Even when he's not looming above me, his sheer size makes me feel so small... so vulnerable.

His pants drop, whispering down his legs, and then he's upon me again, like a hungry animal going in for the kill.

"There are my lips."

His mouth descends on my mouth and his hands push up my bra.

"These are my tits," he growls into my lips.

He gives me one good hard kiss and then his mouth slides down. Grabbing me up, his hands mold around my breasts, squeezing them into his palms.

"Mine," he growls again, and then he's sucking on them. Drawing the tips into his mouth. Suckling noisily on my nipples.

I squirm against the bed, flooded with heat as he makes all these delicious little noises in the back his throat.

"Andrew," I gasp, arching up and clutching at his shoulders as he sucks and sucks, driving me to the brink of madness.

And just when I think I can take no more, he begins to slide down my body, kissing a wet, slippery path.

His tongue circles my bellybutton. "My stomach."

His eyes roll up to stare at me and I draw in my breath in anticipation.

Is he going where I think he's going?

His eyes never leaving me, he slides down my body, his lips dragging over the curve of my mons.

His fingers wrap around my thighs and then he's prying my legs open wider for him.

"This is my sweet little pussy," he rumbles and then his tongue is dragging across my clit.

I jerk as if he just electrocuted me. My muscles tense up and my ass comes off the bed.

He forces me back down with his face.

Pushing his mouth up against my pussy, he sucks me into his mouth and then his tongue starts going crazy. There's no buildup, no time to brace myself, he licks and suckles on me hungrily, like he's trying to devour me with his mouth.

"Oh god," I cry out, my fingers digging into the meaty flesh of his shoulders.

He makes an angry noise in the back of his throat and then his hands spread me wider. His tongue drags up and down my slit, and then he's plunging in, like's he fucking me with it.

"Andrew," I mewl, my core throbbing and aching for him.

In and out, his tongue plunges, but it only leaves me wanting more. Wanting to be filled and stretched by his cock.

"So fucking sweet, so fucking wet," he breathes, his breath hot against my wetness.

The tip of his tongue slithers up and then flicks against my sensitive little clit.

I jerk and twitch.

"So fucking responsive."

His tongue presses against my clit and swirls around and around in tight little circles. Then his fingers slide inside me. Slick with my juices.

He pumps them in and out of me a few times, stretching out my tightness, and then he just stops.

I cry out as his mouth suddenly leaves me. I was so close to coming all over his face but now I'm twitching and trembling like a junkie needing a fix.

"Why did you stop?" I ask, my voice wispy and breathless.

He pulls away and my fingers tighten around his shoulders, trying to keep him from leaving me. He breaks my grip easily and takes a step back.

My hands drop down, defeated to the bed.

Panting, I stare at him, wondering what I did wrong this time.

Is this his punishment? To get me so close and then just stop, leaving me with a pulsing core and a throbbing clit?

"Andrew?"

He grabs me by the hips and then flips me over like it's nothing to him.

"What the fuck?" I cry out and start to push up.

His hand comes down, heavy against my spine and pushes me back down until I'm flat against the mattress.

Once I stop struggling, he grabs me by the hips and drags me down the bed.

I have no clue what he means to do but it's useless trying to fight him. Just trying to push back up was enough to leave me feeling tired and breathless.

His hands fall on my ass, grabbing up two great big handfuls of it.

"This is my ass," he growls and his fingers squeeze, constricting around me.

I moan and arch up into his hands, pushing my face into the mattress.

He shifts behind me and then I feel the heat of his breath brushing over my lower back.

"Mine," he repeats, and then I feel his mouth kissing just where his breath was.

His hands squeeze and squeeze, and he begins to slide down, his lips following.

His right hand moves only to be replaced by his mouth. He kisses and nips at my right cheek while his hand continues to play with the left. Then he's suckling on me and my toes curl against the bed.

Oh my god. I don't know if it feels so good because it's strange and foreign or because I'm extra sensitive there.

He bites me, his teeth sinking into the fleshiest part of my buttock, and then he slides over to do the same to the left.

Just like my breasts, he slides side to side, paying each cheek equal attention. By the time I feel his fingers sliding into my pussy again, I'm nearly delirious with my need for him.

"Andrew, please," I groan, clutching desperately at the sheet on the bed.

"You're still too fucking tight," he grunts, using his fingers to stretch me open.

"I don't care," I whimper. "I want you inside me, *now*."

"Fuck," he grunts, and his fingers pump faster, some of his control starting to slip.

Head falling forward again, I bury my face into the bed, muffling my cries as he uses his fingers to bring me once more to the brink of my orgasm.

I'm so close I can fucking taste it. Then his fingers leave me again.

"Andrew!" I cry out before I feel the head of his cock pushing against my entrance.

"See. Too. Fucking. Tight," he grits out as he fights his way in, pushing through my clench.

Reaching down, he even tries to spread me open but he's just too damn big.

I don't care at this point. I don't care if he fucking rips me open. I need him inside me any way I can get him.

Inch by inch, he pushes his way in. Cursing and praising me for my tightness.

Once he finally bottoms out, I arch my back, pushing my ass into him to take him in even deeper.

"Fuck," he gasps, and I'm wrapped so tightly around him I can feel his cock twitch.

Feeling a deep, visceral kind of satisfaction, I do it again.

"Stop that," he grunts and delivers a sharp smack to my ass.

The pain is so sharp, so surprising, I immediately clamp down on him.

"Fucking hell, you're trying to kill me," he groans and reaches under me, his fingers finding my clit.

Expertly working the little bundle of nerves, he quickly brings me back to the brink of my orgasm, then swiftly sends me soaring over the edge.

I cry out, stars exploding behind my eyes as the walls of my pussy convulse and spasm around him.

"That's better," he grunts with satisfaction, using my gush of wetness to ease the friction.

Pulling back, I still grip him, but I'm too slick to hold him in.

He begins to fuck me slowly at first, easing me open with deep, lingering strokes as if he's truly afraid he might hurt me.

And I enjoy it, savoring every deep stroke of his thick shaft gliding across my g-spot.

But once I come again, trembling and screaming his name, he stops holding back.

He grabs me roughly by the hips, pulls my ass up and begins to fuck me hard and fast.

"Whose pussy is this?" he asks, his thighs driving hard into my ass.

"Yours," I grunt, too far gone to think twice about it.

"That's fucking right," he declares with satisfaction. And then I feel something probing against my other hole.

"And who's ass is this?"

I may be nearly delirious from the pleasure but I'm still aware enough to be a little freaked out as his finger begins to push into me there.

I groan and shake my head, flexing my cheeks and trying to fight against the burning invasion.

"Whose ass is this, Amy?" Andrew hisses and thrusts his finger in.

Hoping my declaration will cause him to pull the finger out, I whimper, "Yours."

He's not satisfied with my answer though.

"Whose?" he grunts, withdrawing his finger only to thrust it back in.

"Yours!" I cry out louder, my ass tightening around his finger. The burning is starting to fade away but I'm still too freaked out to relax.

"That's right," he purrs, finally sounding satisfied and pulling his finger out. "And I'm going to fuck this ass one day... I'm going to mark all of your tight little holes with my dick."

He grabs me by the hair and uses it to arch my head back. "But not today," he breathes into my ear. "Today I'm going to fuck you so hard I'm going to brand this pussy with my cock."

His finger gone, I finally start to relax. But then he wraps my hair around his fist and jerks my head back.

His hips slam into my ass and his skin slaps against my skin.

"And if you forget who you belong to tomorrow, I'll fuck you until you remember."

He begins to fuck me fast and furious.

"I'll fuck you every fucking day until you remember who you belong to."

My body driven forward by the force of his thrusts, I clutch at the bed, only his grip on my hair keeping from topping over.

"I'll fuck you so much you'll be drowning in my cum."

Inside me, I can feel him swelling and growing even larger, and just knowing that he's about to come makes me come again.

I cry out, dropping into warm oblivion, and somehow, someway, he begins to fuck me harder. Faster.

Until he lets out a hair-raising roar.

His warmth begins to fill me then he suddenly pulls out.

I cry out just as spurts of warmth hit my back, then my buttocks.

Slumping forward, I twitch with the last twinges of my orgasm until he presses the head of his cock against the entrance of my ass.

Tensing up again, I whimper as he eases in just enough to fill me there too. Grunting and growling until he's spent.

Slowly he pulls out, and I swear I can feel him wiping

his cock off on my cheeks. But then I fall forward, no longer able to hold myself up.

Catching my breath, I stare at the sheet, trying to figure out just what the fuck happened, and feeling just a little bit violated.

Then Andrew comes down beside me and tips my chin up to look at him.

He grins a slow, very satisfied grin. "You have so much of my cum on you, any man who gets within ten feet of you will be able to smell it."

14

ANDREW

When I was growing up, I never stepped out of line. I never brought attention to myself unless I had done something worthy of it.

In my father's eyes, barely anything was worthy of giving me attention unless it was the back of his hand.

The day I graduated high school was the last day I lived in his house. I was supposed to be a man at that point, and it was deemed I could take care of myself.

Thankfully, I shipped out that week to the military.

There I followed the same rules. I didn't step out of line. I only drew attention to myself through the merit of my actions.

When I joined the Teams, I found a home for the first time. Did I love the Teams? Undoubtedly, but I knew time was fleeting. The lifespan of a Navy Seal isn't in the tens of years, and having my hip torn up by a piece of shrapnel proved that to me.

Getting out of the military and into the life I have now bewilders me. One day I'm fighting terrorists, and the next I'm protecting the life of the devil himself.

Money, and lots of it, that was the start of me working for him. Then came the danger... it still calls to me from time to time.

I think mostly though it was about finding a home. A fucked up home, to be sure.

Lucifer would be the father, with his bitchy wife Simon. The rest of us miscreants are his fucked up little killers.

That's why when Bartholomew betrayed us, I took responsibility for taking his life. He didn't just betray a boss, he betrayed his brothers. I don't see his face in the darkness like I do the others when I sleep at night.

My real parents were cold people, their affections were saved for each other. Not for the brat they brought into the world out of some sense of familial duty. They continued the bloodline, nothing else in their eyes.

I don't know what true love and affection is, I guess. I don't think what I have felt for other women was anywhere near love or care.

Amy and Abigail? I couldn't do without either one of them in my life. I want them here with me. Amy is mine in the most basic sense of the word. Abigail? It's more difficult to describe. I feel a real affection for her. I want the best in the world for her, so to me that means love... I think.

Amy produces a different kind of feeling in me. I feel

it in my chest. It tells me to claim her, to make her mine in every possible way.

To fucking mark her and own her.

"Ready Alpha One and Two, Alpha Three and Five in position," a voice warbles in my ear.

"Go for Alpha One, waiting on Alpha Four," I murmur back.

We've been sitting here in the cold rain for almost two hours waiting for false dawn to start.

"Position Four ready and on high in position," James says through the mic. He's up on a ridgeline with the heavy sniper rifle.

We aren't taking any chances today. This is a shoot to kill job. We'll take prisoners if possible but we don't want to risk a single person escaping.

Checking my cellphone, I send a quick text to Johnathan. "Ready to go. Start time 4:53a.m."

Johnathan quickly responds, "Set to go. 4:53a.m."

We're positioned at two different houses. His is north of the city while mine is to the west of it.

They spread the two hit teams out pretty well, and that's what makes me so damn anxious. I don't like having to do two simultaneous hits at once. But we don't get a choice in this shit. We can't take only one, and we can't hit the second one after we hit the first. Too much could go wrong that way.

Checking my watch, I mark it at 4:51 a.m. "Two minutes."

Each man quickly responds back as we watch the

time count down to a minute before. "Infiltrate. We hit at the 3 mark."

Rushing forward, I keep my barrel up and my finger on the trigger.

My first target is the man leaning against a post with a half-smoked cigarette dangling from his lips. In these early hours of the morning he's half asleep and his night vision is shit from the glowing ember.

Five feet from him, I quietly drop my rifle to its sling and pull the combat knife from my vest. The last few feet are the last moments of his life as I rush to him, slamming the blade into the side of his throat.

A spurt of blood shoots out as I pull the blade from him, hitting me in the chest and face.

Fuck.

Crouching down next to the body, I quietly say, "First position taken. Any issues?"

"Negative. We're still a go, no detection noticeable at this time."

Moving to the corner of the house, I motion to the man who leans up against the brick wall next to the front door. "Get ready to break through the door. Toss a frag grenade in."

Heading back the way I came, I make my way around to the side of the house.

Crouching beneath the bedroom window, I slowly rise up to take a quick peek inside. I see two men sleeping on twin mattresses in a shabby looking room.

"Toss grenades, ten seconds. Enter the front door, sixteen seconds," I murmur into the throat mic.

No whispering shit, whispers carry further than a good murmur.

Two seconds before the toss time, I bust out a portion of the window. The time's up when I drop the grenade through the window. It lands between the alarmed men.

The stunning boom rocks the home as multiple points of the house are breached. Looking back into the room, I see everything is splattered with red, even the black mark of the explosive.

"Alpha One, room clear. Returning to front."

More clears are called as I make my way around. The man at the front of the house has the front door blown wide open and he waits for me to enter first.

Sweeping to the right, I enter the house with one man at my back. We enter the living room where a body is lying prone with blood pooled around the throat. The missing head is my only indication that James has been at work with that sniper rifle of his.

"Living room clear."

"Kitchen clear."

We quickly sweep the rest of the home before taking the stairs.

I'm in lead as I shout up loudly to anyone up there, "We're coming up! Drop all your weapons and you will not be killed!"

There's some scuffling so I murmur to James, "Got a shot on anyone?"

"Switching to thermal," he quietly responds.

Waiting on James, I hear loud shouting and stomping around on the second floor of the house. From the sounds of it they're pissed and want to keep fighting. I wanted to take prisoners if possible, but there's never a good way to tell if someone's too stupid to give up.

"Three warm bodies," James comes back through my earpiece.

"Take 'em out if possible."

"Got it."

I hear a shattering of glass and a loud thump as a body falls to the floor. Five seconds later there's another thump.

Not long after I see a man charging down the stairs with his hands up in the air. He carries no weapon and screams, "Good guy! Good Guy!"

I take a step and stick a foot out to trip him down the rest of the stairs.

"All clear," James comes through the earpiece.

The rest of the men are quick to report the all clear sign.

Just like that, the violence is over and we now have a live body to attend to.

Fuck, this just means paperwork.

WE'RE PACKED up and ready to go. We've cleared the

house of any intel we could find by taking every phone and laptop.

My phone buzzes in my pocket. Lifting it, I press connect. "Job finished, one coming back for questioning."

"Good. Johnathan was able to secure a live one as well. Harrold or his men will be out to clean location soon. Have a couple men stay behind while you bring in the guy," Simon says.

"Got it."

Pointing to James and Marcus, I say, "You two keep watch till Harrold or his men show up."

They nod their heads at me and I head back to the large black Excursion. Climbing in on the driver's side, I shut the door.

Fuck me. I'm wet, cold, and tired as fuck. I still got more work to do though, and I feel like I'm back with the Seals right now.

The only thing that makes it all better is the thought of Amy at home waiting for me to crawl back in bed with her. That and the thought of warming back up by filling her with my cock.

The asshole taped and gagged in the back seat makes a groaning sound. Fuck, night's not over yet.

Driving to the warehouse from here isn't a quick trip. It's pretty much on the opposite side of the city. By the time I reach the building, I'm still wet but hot from the heaters blowing.

I'm only torturing myself though because outside the car the morning is still wet and cold.

Shit.

Stepping out of the car, the cold rain dumps down on my back as I drag the piece of shit from the back. He squirms and tries to fight me but a good punch to the gut knocks some of the fight out of him.

Picking him back up from the puddles in the broken-up parking lot, I slap his face roughly. "Keep it together, asshole."

Thankfully, he doesn't put up much more of a fight until he sees Lucifer standing in the back room of the building.

There's an empty chair bolted to the floor waiting for my bag of shit.

Dumping him on the chair, I chain his ankles to the steel legs and his arms behind his back.

The man is blubbering now. He's so wet I can't tell if he's pissed himself but it sure as fuck smells like it.

Standing up from my work, I unstrap my tactical vest. Hanging it on an old sheet-metal cutting machine, I turn to Simon and Lucifer.

"Good job this morning, Andrew," Lucifer says.

He approaches me as I remove my holster.

"Thanks. Pretty easy in and out job." Pointing to the man screaming in the chair, I say, "He's the only one that surrendered."

"Did you have a chance to question him?" he asks me.

I shake my head. "No, I pulled us out as soon as I got the call from Simon. I didn't want to leave any trace of who took out these guys out."

Extracting my black gloves from my pocket, I start pulling them on.

Lucifer quirks an eyebrow at me.

"My knuckle still gives me issues; these padded puppies help a bit. They also have a hard-outer shell for hitting people with."

Stepping over to the bound man, I look to Simon. "Anything we need specifically, or is this just a general session to get anything we can?"

"Get the full plans of what was supposed to go down tomorrow. Anything else is a bonus at this time."

Nodding my head, I rip the tape off the guy's mouth.

"Talk now," I say to him, "Tell me about the hit on the school tomorrow. This can go on for hours or it can be over quickly. Your choice."

A mouth full of blood and spittle hits my face before I even have a chance to put a hand on him.

Guess that's my cue to start the painful process.

THERE'S NOT a dry bone in my body by the time I make it into the kitchen. My boots make squishing sounds with each step I take.

Amy and Abigail are sitting there at the kitchen table getting ready to start in on cereal and toast.

When they look up at me though I feel like last night was only a dream.

Abigail beams a smile at me.

Amy looks up at me through her long, thick eyelashes and asks, "Are you okay?"

She doesn't ask it like she would have a couple days ago. No, this time there's tenderness in her voice.

"Yeah, let me get cleaned up. You guys in the mood for a big, hot breakfast?"

Abigail looks from me to her mom. Dropping her spoon into her barely-touched bowl of cereal, she asks, "May I have French toast?"

"You sure can, princess. Just let me get showered and dry."

Giggling, Abigail says, "You look like you were in the shower already."

"I bet I do."

Heading out of the kitchen, I keep my hands partially hidden. Even with the gloves on they're bruised with spots of blood.

Grabbing a garbage bag from the utility room, I move up to our bedroom. My shirt under my black jacket isn't wet with only water. Towards the end of the questioning things got a little... bloody.

I don't think either of my girls need to know about that part of my job.

Stripping away the wet layers of clothing, I dump each one into the garbage bag. Everything goes in. My jacket, my black cargo pants, and even my boots.

Nothing from tonight will stay with me. Not the clothes and not the blood.

Naked, I step into the shower.

The stinging hot water washes all the blood and grime down the drain, leaving no trace of the violence I inflicted.

15

AMY

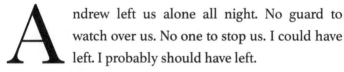ndrew left us alone all night. No guard to watch over us. No one to stop us. I could have left. I probably should have left.

But something held me back.

I want to tell myself I was too afraid to walk out the door because of Ivan. He was released yesterday and I know he's out there, somewhere. Waiting.

But it wasn't only Ivan. Something else is holding me here. Something that sits heavy in my chest. Something that continues to grow, like a cancer.

Instead of leaving or plotting an escape, I stayed up most of the night wondering where Andrew was.

What was he doing? Was he with Lucifer? Was he killing people?

Or was he with another woman?

I shouldn't care, I shouldn't, but I do. The mere

thought of him with someone else makes me so angry I could cry.

I truly have no control of this situation. He can do whatever he wants, whoever he wants.

It's not like we're in a healthy relationship here.

I hated him for not telling me where he was going, or what he was doing. I hated him for making me feel this way. For making feel anything in the first place. It's fucking insane.

Insane.

But as soon as he walked in the door, soaked to the bone and smelling faintly of blood, I didn't want to know where he was or what he was doing.

And the sick, fucked-up part of me was glad he was finally home.

I'm in over my head here, and the water is only getting deeper.

Beside me, Abigail squirms in her chair, glancing towards the TV. Knowing she has French toast coming her way she's no longer interested in the cereal.

"Go watch some TV," I smile at her. "You're excused from the table."

She flashes me a bright smile and darts out of her chair.

I stand up and clean up the bowls of cereal. I take my time dumping them out and washing them by hand, waiting for Andrew to come back downstairs.

When he doesn't, I decide to go up and check on him.

The smell of minty soap and steamy water greets me as I push open the bedroom door.

"Andrew?" I call out. "Are you okay?"

When he doesn't answer, I decide I better check. Who knows what kind of shit he got up to last night.

Maybe he smelled like blood because he was bleeding?

I step inside the bedroom and immediately have to step over a big black garbage bag left on the floor. *That's odd*, I think.

I nudge the bag open and the coppery smell of blood wafts out. I quickly nudge the bag closed again, deciding I really don't want to know what's in there.

"Andrew?" I call out again, walking up to the bathroom door.

Still no answer.

Fearing that he's hurt, I push the door open.

"Andrew?" I call out, trying to peer through the thick cloud of steam.

Still, he doesn't answer me.

I step inside the bathroom and walk up to the shower door. Through the foggy glass I can make out his large silhouette. It looks like he's still standing. Maybe he just didn't hear me?

"Andr—"

The shower door opens and I'm yanked inside.

I start to squeal as the water hits me but a hand immediately covers my mouth.

"Shush," he murmurs. "You don't want to alarm Abigail."

He pushes me up against the shower wall and stares down into my eyes.

I blink the water from my lashes and peer up at him.

Slowly, he begins to pull his hand away.

"What are you doing?" I whisper up at him. "My clothes are completely soaked now."

He looks down, his dark gaze warming as it roams over me slowly, almost lazily. His lips begin to curve into a smile. "You're right, they're soaked."

He grabs the bottom of my shirt and tugs it up.

"Wait..." I hiss but he doesn't stop. Pulling the shirt over my head, he tosses it carelessly to the side where it lands with a wet plop.

"Why did you do that?" I frown.

His mouth comes down on my mouth. His hands pull down my bra straps.

I reach up, trying to stop him but his mouth keeps slanting over my mouth, driving me to distraction.

His kiss deepens, his lips pulling hungrily from my lips as my bra falls away. One warm, slick hand comes down on my right breast, squeezing it, while the other shoves down my pajama pants.

"Andrew," I moan into his mouth. "We shouldn't..."

"Shush," he growls and kisses me harder to keep me quiet.

His knee nudges at my knee and then he reaches down, pulling my leg up, hooking it on his hip.

Groaning into my mouth, he pushes forward, filling me up with his hard cock.

I throw my head back. He's so deep and I'm so full, I feel like he just pinned me to the damn wall.

He pulls out slowly and immediately thrusts forward.

A little sound escapes my lips.

His hand slaps over my mouth.

"Be quiet," he hisses.

I try, I really do, but it's so hard to be quiet as he begins to fuck me like the end of the world is coming.

His wet body slams into my body like he's trying to slam me through the tile. And he drives himself so hard, so deep, the power behind his thrusts forces me up on my toes.

I claw at his back, at his sides, and at his shoulders, desperately trying to find something to hold on to, but he's too slick and too wet for me to find purchase.

My hands just end up sliding all over him.

"Come for me," he growls into my ear, and to my horror I feel my body begin to respond to his command.

My mind protests the submission but my core pulses and the pressure inside me expands.

"Come for me, Amy," he growls again, and then his teeth latch onto my neck.

He drives into me harder and deeper. Smashing my ass against the wall.

"Andrew," I groan behind his hand and his grip tightens.

His cock drives extra deep and he smashes my clit.

I jerk against him, crying out his name again.

Teeth releasing my neck, he hisses, "I said be quiet."

His hand slides up, covering my nose and cutting off my air.

I can't breathe. Desperately, I try to pull in oxygen but I'm being smothered by the palm of his hand.

I try to fight him, I try to shove him off but he's too strong, too determined.

His body slams into my body again and again.

Spots flash in front of my eyes.

I'm dying.

Suffocating.

But amazingly my orgasm is still building.

"I said *come*," he grunts into my ear and I explode.

My nose burns and my lungs ache, but the orgasm that rocks through my body is extra strong. Colors overtake the spots flashing in front of my eyes, and warm, wet waves roll through my core.

I think the lack of oxygen may be enhancing my release.

The pleasure feels twice as strong as usual and there's this strange rush flooding through my nerves.

"Yes," he grunts quietly as I clamp down on him. "That's a *good girl*."

I feel him swell up, growing inside me, then he's grinding himself slow and deep as he fills me up with his warmth.

Just when I'm about to pass out, he removes his hand and I gasp in a mouthful of much needed air.

He holds me tightly as I twitch and spasm on top of his cock. Catching my breath and still coming at the same time.

As soon as the last tremor fades and I get some of my strength back, I push him away.

Our eyes meet.

Mine are confused and hazy.

His are warm and tender.

"You almost killed me," I hiss.

He smirks and tucks an errant strand of my hair behind my ear. "If I wanted to kill you—" he starts but he's cut off as Abigail calls out.

"Mommy? Andrew?"

It sounds like she's in the bedroom.

"Just a minute, honey!" I call out in a panic. "Mommy's in the bathroom!"

"Oh, okay!" she responds cheerfully with some relief.

I wonder how long she's been wondering about me.

"I might be awhile... Wait for me downstairs."

"Oh... Okay!" she calls back less enthusiastically.

I hold my breath, listening closely to her walk out of the bedroom. A moment later we can hear her skipping down the stairs.

"Good grief," I groan and slump against the wall. "That was too close."

"It was," Andrew agrees, frowning thoughtfully. "I think it's time she went back to school."

16

ANDREW

S hit. I've never been a thinker really. I mean, when have I ever needed to? It was always go here, shoot that, remove this.

Now I'm sitting here in Simon's pristine office and my head is spinning in circles. I'm the caveman type. I don't do the whole going through all the facts and investigating things shit.

"That's all that we have. They were paid for the job through a blind contract, but they knew it would be for the Russians. No connections to them though. The guys who've been identified were all hitters out of Russia, Ukraine, and one from Syria," Simon recites to me off of the notepad on his desk.

I lift my eyebrows at him, that just doesn't seem right. "They're all contractors? No actual mafia men?"

"None that we could get a line on. You did get the

prints off of all the ones at your site?" he asks, and I swear he's trying to fuck with me.

He knows for a fact I do my job to the letter. I don't leave shit out.

"You have the thumb and forefinger off of every guy there, Simon. What the hell do you want me to do? Start snipping them off next and bring them to you?"

Johnathan starts to rumble a gravelly laugh beside me. "Can you see the Spider with a baggy of removed digits?"

Seriously, I don't find this shit funny at all. Simon is missing something from our raids and I can feel how bad it is. We missed someone or something. Either Johnathan or I did. I just don't know what, and Simon doesn't either.

Elbowing Johnathan in the ribs, his laugh dims down to a low chuckle. "Shut the fuck up for a second, biker boy. Think about it... When have you ever known the Russians to hire out something like this?"

"It's a snatch and grab. They—" he starts.

"No, no, no. Listen to me, John, it wasn't just that," I growl out.

My head's spinning and I can see Simon watching me out of the corner of my eye. He's been following this same path that I'm going down and he doesn't like the end result, if there is one.

"Let's go back a bit, like to the Yakuza hit on Lucifer's wife."

That shuts them both up and I can tell I have their full attention.

"She's snatched and we went charging in to bring her back. We put a call out to all of the city's hitters to get that operation done. Right?"

Johnathan shrugs but Simon nods his head slowly. "We did. We even put a bounty in with the Russians."

"Right. What the fuck did that do for us? We got three guys, two of which swore they were just some fry cooks from a local restaurant. Why the fuck didn't the Russians cash in with all the fleeing bastards? I mean, seriously, even our guys were pulling in tattooed bastards daily. Lucifer shelled out almost a hundred mil, right?"

"I wish he hadn't put that bounty out there like that... It was... reckless," Simon says.

"The Russians didn't do shit. That's odd. They need money too, ya know? Then with Bart I get some answers on names. We hear Ivan's name but that's it. Everyone who was in the know spilled a ton of shit to us, but no one knew who the financial backers were."

"So the Russians and the Yakuza are in the same boat. We know that..." Johnathan grunts.

He's right, this is becoming fairly easy to prove knowledge. Except the Russians are staying quiet, they aren't banging on our door for Ivan. Why the fuck not? He's worth a shit ton of money and he had knowledge of the job to get Lucifer's kids.

So we knocked off their teams. From the weapons and intel we pulled from the house, they were going for the kids, but to what end?

"Something's missing from this whole shit-storm.

Like what are they playing at? Is this just a job from the Yakuza? Retribution for what we did to their operations?"

"Now you see why I asked if anyone was missing. It's not like the Russians to do a job like this without some of their connected men in on the operation."

Simon has his fingertips steepled together in front of his face. His eyes are watching us both like a spider getting ready to snap us up.

"So you think we missed someone or something?" Johnathan asks.

"It's crossed my mind, and Lucifer's. We both agree a puzzle piece is missing, but... We don't know what it is."

"You think we fucked up that bad or you thinking we're rats?" Johnathan asks as he scoots forward in his chair.

Rolling his eyes, Simon says, "No, we have no doubts as to your loyalties."

Nodding his head, Johnathan says, "Then what the fuck are you getting at?"

Watching the byplay, I can see the faint dark circles around Simon's eyes. He's tired and stressed.

This isn't normal for him.

Simon is nothing if not a completely detached professional. He doesn't deal in emotions or feelings. He's one of the analytical elites. He deals with data, numbers, and intel. If I hadn't seen him get stabbed once in the leg, I would think he was a fucking robot.

He's so fucking collected, calm, and disgusted by dirt. He has contacts that reach across the world, and that's why they call him the Spider. It's not a name said in good humor either. If he's got someone in his web, they're as good as dead.

If Simon isn't connecting the dots... fuck.

"How sure are we that this is something?" I ask, trying to get between the two before tempers flare.

Simon's eyes wander back to me. "We aren't."

"Bullshit. My hackles are raised now just as much as yours."

Johnathan slumps back into his chair.

"Too much is not happening," I say.

"Where's Ivan? What's our info say about him?"

"He's gone to ground. Ghosted our men as soon as he got out," Simon says with a wince.

"What the fuck do you mean he ghosted? Where the fuck is he?" I nearly yell.

"From the whispers I got, he and the wife have been taken back to the motherland. To answer some tough questions."

"Are you fucking with me?" I ask.

"No, that's what we figured would happen after the raids. Looks like they want to know how word got out about those two little groups."

"Well, fuck," I say. "I still don't like any of this. It's too easy."

Simon shrugs his shoulders and frowns. "I've got feelers out on the ground right now. I need you guys to keep an ear out."

Nodding my head, I look down at my watch. "I need

to go up and talk to the boss. He wants to know how my girl is doing in her new school with Evelyn."

Simon rolls his eyes and starts rubbing his temples. He emits a long sigh. "Yes, let's just put a hold on things so we can discuss the women in your lives."

Laughing loudly, Johnathan holds out his fist to Simon. "Not going to trap us, brother! Fucking leeches, all of 'em. Soon as they can they get their claws in ya, they get you turned around so much you don't know where your balls went."

If anything, Simon looks disgusted by Johnathan. I can practically see the revulsion Simon feels at the thought of touching skin with a biker.

"What? I washed my hands a couple of hours ago, ya fucking priss."

Simon turns in his chair, away from us both, before waving a hand in our direction. "I'll call when I know more."

We both stand and walk out of the office, towards the elevators.

Pushing the up button, I look over at Johnathan. "You really like pushing his buttons, don't you?"

"Fuck yeah. Dude's so uptight, I bet he turns lumps of coal into diamonds in his spare time by shoving them up his ass."

Shaking my head, I say, "Yeah, well, he probably still considers you a knuckle-dragging Neanderthal."

"Someone's gotta be the muscle in this place."

17

ANDREW

I f this was a movie, it's right now, as I'm pulling into the garage, that I would have some big fucking breakthrough thought about all that's going on around us.

I don't get it though. It's been a busy two weeks since I spoke with Simon. The city has gone from a hornet's nest of activity to absolute quiet.

Nothing is happening—no wars, no violence, no tension. The world it seems is going on with life. Everything is normal. We've got Abigail in school, been house shopping, clothes shopping, grocery shopping...

Shopping out my fucking ears.

I don't like the normal. Normal is the bad part. Normal is when the villain springs a trap on the unsuspecting adventurer. It's like the longer things go on in life like nothing happened, the worse I know the next event is going to be.

Fuck, I hate the waiting.

And life around the house has been getting a little crazy. We've gone from me having to keep my girls in the house, safe and sound, to getting them out in the real world again.

Amy was scared shitless when I told her Ivan was gone. She doesn't like the thought of him being alive any more than I do, I think. She hasn't said anything, but I can tell she wishes I had taken that fucker's life. Taken the man who threatened her and her daughter. I wish I had. Fuck the consequences.

I'd like to kill that fuck like the pig he is.

Amy's been coming out of her shell bit by bit. The news of Ivan being released terrified her, but she knows she's mine now. She has nothing to worry about.

And every night I try to drill that into her mind and body.

She's not going to be simply a wife to me or the woman who warms my bed. No, she's my possession.

My fucking obsession.

Mine down to the very core of her being.

I can't even stand the thought of anyone else coming near her, smelling her, or touching her.

There's an inky blackness that surrounds my mind. What we have consumes me. It burns like a fire raging through my soul.

Amy represents something to me that I will never have. Something I've never touched before. Something inheritably good and pure. She's so beautiful to me, so fucking ethereal, that it can be painful to think of for any length of time.

She's the good side of the darkness that I bring to the world. She has a fucking halo, not the horns I wear.

I'm not a good guy. I kill people and I don't feel bad about it. I've done and seen things I should never have, but her light tugs at my soul.

I shouldn't allow myself to be drawn to the sun, but I have no choice. The more I watch her, the more I must have her. The more I must hoard her.

She is the corner of the universe I want to keep to myself.

Stepping out of the new smelling car, I grin widely. It's a thing of beauty. Cost an arm and a leg, but it's worth it.

Fuck, for half a million dollars, this thing better see Abigail through high school. Not that it will, I plan on my girls and unborn child having the best they can.

If that means dipping into the considerable nest egg I've built up over the past few years, then so be it.

Leaning my head into the kitchen from the garage, I shout, "Hey sex-on-a-stick, get out here!"

"What did you just call me?" Amy all but shrieks across the house to me.

"Come here, I have a present for you," I say as she comes into the kitchen. The annoyed look on her face gives me a chuckle. She hates it when I objectify her.

"Why?" she asks me.

"Because I want the best for you. There's no trap in

my presents, Amy. You're safe with me," I say before ducking back out of the doorway.

I haven't closed the garage door and the sunlight streaming in from the outside shows off how sparkly the new car is.

Eyes wide as can be, she takes a step into the garage. I toss the key to her but I guess she's not paying too much attention because it bounces off her chest and drops to the floor.

"What do you mean a present for me?" she asks as she eyes the car.

Pointing to the car, I say, "A present, as in a gift, to the mother of my children. You know, the woman I keep claiming in the bedroom every night?"

I walk over to her and bend over to pick up the key. Straightening, I wrap an arm around her and help her walk around the car as I slip the key into her hand.

"This is yours. You're going to need something safe to drive around in when you are dress shopping for the wedding."

She stops at the word wedding, pushing the key back into my hand. "What do you mean wedding?"

"We're going to be married, Amy. You're the mother of my unborn child. You are the mother of my daughter Abigail."

"I have a say in these things! And Abigail isn't your daughter! I'm probably not even pregnant!" she shouts.

She pushes the key back into my hand and starts backing away from me.

Taking two large steps to her, I grab her hand and yank her back to the car.

Spinning her around, I bend her over the car's still warm engine hood.

My hand comes down in a solid whap three times. Each time it connects with her bottom I hear her breath gasp out.

"Fight it all you want, Amy, but you need to come to the realization that you're fucking *mine*. You're pregnant with my child. And nothing, and I mean *nothing,* is going to change that. You can fight this all you want, but if you yell at me like that again, I'm going to start treating you like an obstinate child."

Pulling her back up, I look her hard in the eyes. "You could've had a say in these things if you hadn't put yourself in the position you did. I told you once, be a good girl and I would keep you safe. I've kept my word on that. I will never allow you to be hurt again. Not by anyone. You're fucking mine. Do we need a reminder of that?"

Shaking her head, she doesn't speak. I don't know if it's the spanking or the vehemence in my voice... It's probably a mixture of them both leaving her mute as she stares at me.

Leaning in, I rest my forehead against hers. "You need to give up the silly notion you're not pregnant. It's a fact."

She shakes her head again and turns away from me. "How can you be so certain?"

"Because, like that night in the limo when I chose to

take you as mine, I know that you're pregnant. I know it in here," I say pointing to my chest.

It's a bold statement, but it's true. Pressing my lips against hers, I hold her to me. I won't stop until she's panting.

Her hands push at me as always. Always fighting my little angel is. Always fighting the demon whose stolen her.

Slowly those soft lips of hers part and her breath comes out in short little bursts as my tongue skims across her own. Melting in my arms, she allows me to pull her tight to my body.

When we finally stop, I force myself to not push her over the engine hood again. Force myself to not thrust my cock into her achingly tight pussy.

Rolling my shoulders, I step back and smile. "That's the angel I know. Now let's look at your new car."

She shakes her head and says, "It's way too much, Andrew..."

I growl at her and resist the urge to spank her again. "No, it's not. This is for your safety and I won't skimp on that. This car is armored against most bullets. I want you three as safe as possible when you start driving Abigail to school."

She nods her head hesitantly and squeezes my hand. Then her trembling fingers take the key fob I hold out to her.

I nudge her towards the shiny silver S550 Benz.

She looks at the car, then back at me like she just can't believe it. I nod at her and keep nudging her.

After sliding behind the wheel and getting comfortable, she finally cracks a smile.

That smile fills my chest with warmth.

I'm happy with my life, I think, and that worries the fuck out me.

18

AMY

Is it possible to fall in love with someone just because they fuck you a lot? Because if it is, then I'm totally fucked.

No pun intended.

These past few weeks it feels like that's all Andrew and I have done. We take care of Abigail, get her off to school, then start fucking.

On the kitchen counter. In the backseat of the car.

Up against the wall in the garage.

We've even snuck in a few quickies in the houses we've been looking at.

You'd think by now we'd start to get tired of each other, that we'd get our fill. But this lust, this craving I have for Andrew only seems to be getting worse. The sickness inside of me is spreading.

It's no longer a simple matter of just giving into the attraction growing between us.

It's turning into a real need.

I *need* to have him inside me. I *need* to feel his skin against my skin. To feel his teeth sinking into my neck, marking me.

On a daily basis.

There's a safety in being his. There's a rightness to it.

And it's terrifying.

I can't rely on him, I can't... To do so would be giving up, and I'm not ready to give up yet. There's still a chance that Abigail and I can get away from all this madness. From these men who rule the world with their money and viciousness.

There's still a chance I'm not pregnant.

"What are you doing?" I ask Lily.

She's scrunching up her face and squinting her eyes at me.

I walked into her room a moment ago but I know she's been expecting me. We planned this days ago.

"I'm trying to tell if you're pregnant."

"You look like you're constipated and trying to take a shit," I tell her.

She tips her head back and laughs. And nearly tumbles off her bed. I quickly grab her, tugging her back up, and she instantly sobers.

"Why were you looking at me like that?" I ask once she's got her balance back.

Wiping the tears from her eyes, she says, "I was trying to open my third eye."

"Huh?" I frown at her, still not getting it.

She sighs and leans away. "This old Japanese guy once told me you could tell a lot about someone if you looked closely enough."

"Okay," I nod my head, not sure what else to say. It sounds utterly ridiculous.

She smiles sheepishly at me. "Yeah, now that I think about it, it seems really silly... It was probably just a lucky guess."

"What was?"

"Oh, nothing," she waves her hand in the air, dismissively.

Sensing she wants to drop the matter, I ask, "Well?"

She drops her hand and blinks at me. "Well, what?"

Fuck. She must have forgot it. With everything going on, it must have slipped her mind...

"Oh!" She exclaims and her face lights up. "I got it."

She scoots off the end of the bed and then dashes to her closet. A moment later she's rushing back over to me, waving a small rectangular box in the air.

Seeing the box, I experience a moment of relief that she didn't forget. Then that relief morphs into sheer, paralyzing terror.

This is it. The moment of truth.

What if I am?

What if I'm not?

Taking in the look on my face, Lily's steps slow and she seems to hesitate.

"Are you sure?" she asks, holding the box back.

I know if I decide to back out, she'd totally understand. That's why I like hanging out with her so much. There are no hard questions and there's no judgment.

I take a deep, fortifying breath and say, "I'm sure."

Lily passes the box over to me.

I grip it tightly in my hand, nearly crushing it, as we walk over to the bathroom.

"You know," she says, swinging open the bathroom door for me. "Whatever happens, I'm here for you."

I offer her a faint smile and nod my head. I march inside like I'm marching to my death. "Thank you."

She smiles back at me and closes the door for me.

I look down at the box in my hand.

Now it's just the pregnancy test and me.

Please... Please, if there's anyone up there, don't let me pregnant, I begin to pray.

It's been six weeks since they grabbed me. It feels like it's been a lifetime but it's only been six short weeks.

Weeks that were filled with unprotected sex.

I haven't had my period. I'm actually four weeks late. But there's still a chance it's because of all the stress I've been through. This has happened before. I skipped my period once when I was afraid I wouldn't be able to make rent.

Please, please, please.

I repeat after peeing on the end of the stick.

I'd give anything...

One line darkens.

I'll be a good girl...

Then two.

Fuck.

I grab up the little cardboard box. My eyes scroll over the instructions.

One line—negative.

Two lines—positive.

I jump up and yank the door open.

Lily jumps back and I thrust the little stick at her.

"I think it's broken."

She glances down at the stick but doesn't take it. Looking back up at me, her smile is sympathetic. "It's very rare to get a false positive."

That is not what I wanted to hear.

I stare at her and her smile wavers. "How long has it been since your last period?"

Amazingly, I have to think about it. Maybe because I was purposely *not* thinking about it.

"It was two weeks before I was grabbed…"

It's been eight weeks! Eight fucking weeks since the last time I had my period.

"Shit," I whisper and feel a crushing weight settling on my chest.

Why is this happening to me? What did I do to deserve this? I can't spend the rest of my life with him. I don't want to be permanently chained to him.

He doesn't love me. It's something darker. Something deeper.

More primal.

A need to control and possess.

That's destroying me in the process.

I don't know who I am anymore. I don't know what I want, what I need.

"What am I going to do?"

Lily stares at me helplessly.

I thought... *No*, I hoped that if I just willed it hard enough, I wouldn't conceive. That my will was stronger than his.

I should have known better. Even in this, he's stronger than me.

There's only one thing I can do.

"Lily, you have to help me," I plead.

She smiles at me but her eyes are instantly wary. "Of course. What do you need?"

"You need to help me get away."

"Are you sure you want to do that?" She frowns. "I know you're in shock, but you should really think about this..."

I laugh at her, balancing on the razor edge of hysteria. "All I've done is think about this. Are you going to help me or not?"

Lily shifts and sighs, her brow furrowing as she thinks it over. She glances towards the door as if she expects someone to come through it at any moment. Then she walks up to me, grabs me by the arm and leads me back into the bathroom.

"I'm probably the only person who *can* help you," she whispers while shutting the door behind us.

I nod my head at her, instantly relieved that she's not going to try to talk me out of it.

"Where do you want to go?" she asks.

"Anywhere away from here," I automatically answer.

She nods her head. "Okay. But where? You need a specific destination."

I think for a moment. I could go to my aunt... but Andrew already mentioned that's the first place he would look for me.

I shake my head helplessly. "I don't know. Anywhere..."

"Do you have any relatives?" Lily asks, her sympathy growing by the second. "Anyone who will hide you?"

"I don't have any other relatives. My grandparents passed before I was born, and my parents passed in a car accident when I was eighteen months old," I explain. "I'd have to start somewhere new. Somewhere completely by myself."

My aunt raised me but she only did it out of necessity. I don't think she resented me but she wasn't anything like a mother to me.

I've never had a real family.

And now that I think about it, neither will my children. Abigail's father completely abandoned her when she was a baby. To him she was just a teenage mistake.

And this baby...

Their father will probably never stop hunting me. We'll always be running.

Because he wants them... Because he wants me.

Oh god.

He wants us. For the first time I'm actually wanted.

"Are you sure you want to do this?" Lily asks hesitantly.

I shake my head, my composure cracking. "No."

I'm not sure. I have no clue what I want anymore...

"Oh honey," Lily sighs, stepping up to me and giving me a hug.

The comfort is the last big crack in my wall. The tears come and the shudders start.

I cry because of all the things I can't change. I cry because of all the things I can.

I cry because Andrew is better at taking care of us and protecting us than I ever was.

I cry even harder because last night, before bed, Abigail called him daddy when he tucked her in.

And god help me, I think I'm in love with him, and I think I want to stay with him...

Bzzt. *Bzzt, Bzzt.*

"Shit, hold on, Amy," I say as my cock just barely grazes her juicy pussy lips.

The throbbing from my thick monster is driving me nuts. Just being so near her body like this is driving me mad.

Bzzt. Bzzt. Bzzt.

Yanking my pants up from where they were pooled at my feet, I growl as I paw through my pockets. Grabbing my phone, I see that it's Paul calling.

Fuck.

What now? He should be guarding the school where Abigail and Evie are at. What the fuck now? Did some teacher try hitting on him again?

Swiping to connect, I put the phone to my ear.

Looking into Amy's eyes, I watch the heat in them flare as I edge the tip of my cock back into her folds. She's giving me that feral grin, the one that dares me to break her.

"Paul this bett—" I start to say before being quickly cut off by his cracking voice.

There are gunshots in the background and I hear automatic rifles going off.

"They're hitting the school again! There's at least ten men!"

My throbbing cock instantly goes soft as the words he's shouting in my ear register. Amy gives me questioning look.

Pulling back, I start yanking my pants up, fastening the top button up.

"Where are the girls?" I yell into the phone as I rush out of the kitchen towards the garage. Amy is hot on my heels as I all but break through the door to the garage.

In the background I hear someone screaming, "In there, in there!"

"I've got them in the office with me, but they are breaching! Panic button was hit before I called you!"

Shit, shit, shit!

Yanking open the car door, I throw myself inside. Amy is in the passenger seat before I even have a chance to tell her to stay. One look at her and I know it's useless.

There's a loud explosion and then I hear Paul shouting for the girls to stand behind him. There's a lot of gunfire, way too much.

Static and gunfire.

Fuck.

Slamming into reverse, we just barely miss ripping the garage door off its track. I punch the button to close it back up as I race backward, down the driveway.

I feel my stomach drop as the phone switches from only audio in my ear to coming through the Bluetooth in the car. Every gunshot is heard in crystal clear definition.

Amy's eyes are wide as she screams out, "What's happening!?"

"Hold on! We're going there now!"

The Mercedes may be an armored car but its engine still packs a huge punch when I slam down on the gas. We rocket down the street at an incredible pace. It won't be fast enough though, gunfights like this only last five minutes tops.

It'll take twenty to get to the school.

"Paul!" I shout in the phone repeatedly but get nothing.

Only gunfire.

Then all of a sudden there is nothing but silence.

Silence fades as footsteps and the loud screams of the girls come through the phone.

Shit. They have the girls. They have Abigail.

Amy is hysterical by the time I hang up the phone. We've been listening to static for almost two minutes.

Dialing Simon quickly, I shout as soon as he answers, "I'm fifteen minutes out! What's the situation?"

"Give me a second, Andrew. The hit team is in a fire fight against our guys outside of the school."

I try to be patient, I really do. But five minutes in I start yelling at Simon that I need information.

"They've blasted through our guys. Hurry up and get to the school, Andrew. We need you on the ground. Lucifer is on his way with Johnathan. They've taken one of the girls, it's not sure who. The other has been hurt. Get there now. I'll contact you with more information if I can get it."

Fuck me. They took Evie and hurt Abigail. Shit

My hand must be crushing Amy as I grip it with my fears of not being able to protect my girls.

For her part, Amy is sitting there in shock. No words are escaping her mouth as she just opens and closes it.

WHEN WE FINALLY GET TO the school, police cars and firetrucks have us blocked out. I call Johnathan though and he has our car escorted inside the taped-off area.

We come to a halt in front of an ambulance.

Looking over to the Amy, I say, "It's okay, baby. We'll be okay."

Getting out of the car, we both race to the ambulance. My heart is thudding in my chest as I think of only this morning when Abigail said she loved me before jumping out of the car.

She's been doing that for a few days now. Every morning I drop her off and she says, "Love you, Daddy."

She's accepted me into her world, and for once in my

life I feel like I might actually have a heart and soul after all.

As we round the back of the ambulance, I see Johnathan standing next to a very angry looking Lucifer. Anger shouldn't be his only reaction; he should be murderous if someone took his Evelyn, right?

The little girl laying on the stretcher is beneath a blanket, her little red princess slippers peeking out from underneath it.

Red slippers. Abigail wore yellow ones today.

Ivan.

Turning back to face Amy, I wrap her tightly in my arms.

Holding her as tight as I can, I say, "Baby, that's not Abby."

"What... what do you mean? They took Evie, not my Abigail!" she screams at me.

Then, without me being able to hold her tight enough, she spins around to see a bruised and battered Evie curled up on the stretcher.

There's a loud scream of pure terror that ends just as fast as it begun. Amy goes limp in my arms and her eyes roll back into her head as she passes out.

Carefully sweeping her up into my arms, I walk over to the EMTs.

"Help," I whisper.

∾

Johnathan has been taking care of Amy in the ambulance. She woke up and has gone into a silent shock. When I ask him to escort her home and to watch over her, he doesn't even bat an eye.

Nodding his head, he helps her to his black Expedition.

Johnathan seems to be in a state of his own. I know the man liked Abigail, and it's obvious from the look on his face that her being taken is weighing heavily on him.

I walk over to Lucifer.

He pulls away from a sobbing Evelyn long enough to say, "They took Abigail. From what I can tell, they had no interest in Evelyn. When she tried to stop them they beat her up pretty good. They *asked* for Abigail."

Nodding my head, I say, "I'll get with the police and start questioning some of the staff. Where's Paul?"

"He went down throwing his body over the girls. That's where most of the blood on Evelyn came from."

Fuck. They fucking took Abigail. It's fucking Ivan, the fucking ghost who's come back to haunt us.

Growling at Lucifer, I say, "It was fucking Ivan."

"That's my guess, as well. Ask around here quickly. I'm having Simon work on where he went. We will get what we need soon."

I look long and hard at Lucifer. Long and hard. We could have had Ivan; this could have been avoided. My daughter's life is in jeopardy because of his bad fucking decision.

"We're going to need to talk, Lucifer. This shouldn't

have fucking happened."

Nodding his head, he says, "Agreed. But for the time being we must focus all of our efforts on fixing the current situation."

Walking away from him, I head to the police officers who are corralling the teachers hanging around the school entrance. There is a mixture of our armed men, the police, and staff there.

An officer is shouting loudly, "All teachers, please keep your students in their rooms. Soon, we'll allow the parents to collect their children. Please report if any student is missing from your class. Now please head back to your rooms. Keep the children calm."

The teachers mill about for a moment before I roar out, "Go to your classrooms now!"

I'm not in the mood for stupid people right now and they need to be professionals. They need to be able to protect the children like I couldn't do.

After questioning a couple of officers about what happened, I head towards the room where Paul made his last stand.

We have the money in this town, we own the police. They don't bat an eye when I start moving about.

Stepping into the room where the standoff happened, I kneel in front of a body Paul took down with him. From the looks of it, he did more than his share of killing. He took down six guys.

Six.

That's a lot of men to kill while protecting two children and yourself.

Flipping over the bodies, I rip open shirts and check their hands. They have tattoos all over their chests and hands. Russian prison tattoos. These are the real deal when it comes to a Russian hit squad. These are the heavy hitters we should have originally been facing.

This was the loose end we couldn't find.

Beside Paul, I sit down for a moment. Another brother is gone from our family now. This one died protecting us.

Too many holes fill him. The scene around him, the spent cartridges... he didn't protect himself in the end. It's obvious he gave no thought to himself, it was all for the girls.

Closing his eyes, I try not to allow myself to feel the deep down inferno of rage wanting to unleash inside of me. I need to be cool and calm right now; I need to collect information, not become a beacon of anger.

Shaking my head, I stand up from his body with the hope that the men he took with him will be his slaves in the next life.

Loud voices pierce through my fog as I leave the room. The office across from the one I was in looks almost pristine compared to the one I was in. Inside of it, I see two officers speaking with the principal of the school.

Stopping just outside of the door, I hear him say, "This wouldn't have happened if these cretins would keep their children away from my school! But I get no say in the filth that comes through the doors. The board allows donors to bring their little brats here if they give enough."

My tongue feels thick in my mouth, the bile that is rising from my guilt of Abigail being taken is quickly becoming rage. How dare he call my daughter *filth*.

Walking past one of the officers, I move directly in front of the small, sniveling man. He's a short, fat, balding little fuck. When Amy and I arranged for Abigail to come to school, he gave us trouble and now he's insulting her.

Grabbing his wrist, I yank him forward as I growl out, "Do not insult my girl!"

"Officer! Officers! Get him off me!" he screams to the two uniformed men and the detective.

That scream. That fucking scream causes me to stop. My hand locks on his wrist as I say, "I recognize your scream…"

The police are trying to pull me off the guy as I say, "Scream for me one more time, scream *'In there'*."

They have me off him, but the man has gone from indignant red to a very pale shade of green. "What… you must be mad… get him away from me."

Eyeing the detective, I say, "Make him scream it."

Looking from me to the police, the principal's eyes go wide. "Now, see here! You're the law, he can't…"

None of the officers make a sound or movement as I pull my .45 out of my holster and aim it at the man's knee. "Scream it now."

"In there!" he screams out. "In there! In there!"

That's the voice I heard through the phone, this is my daughter's Judas.

Looking back to the police, I say, "He told the hit squad where my daughter was hiding."

Looking back and forth at each other, the officers start to go for the man before I shake my head. "I'll deal with him. You guys go find another person to question."

It's a sign of how much Lucifer controls this city now that the police officers turn away from me and the blubbering man. They know right now there's not a single thing they can do to stop me.

At a time like this there isn't a pocket we can't grease.

Grabbing the man by the shirt, I yank his tie loose then up and over his head. Cramming the ugly silk piece of shit into his mouth, I silence most of the wailing that was coming out. I slap the side of my pistol against his head and watch his eyes get hazy.

Holstering the .45, I head out of his office, yanking him with me.

Pulling my phone from my pocket, I quickly dial Simon. "What is it?"

"I'm taking care of the principal. Little fucking prick told the hit squad where the girls were at."

"Fucks sake, are you serious?" he asks quietly.

"Yeah."

"I'll inform Lucifer. Go ahead and get any information you can. I'll smooth anything over with the police."

"Hurry up with the smoothing over, FBI just pulled up on the scene."

"Will do."

Dragging the man into one of our guy's black SUV, I say, "Get a ride with someone else. I need to take this one in."

It's three quick punches that knock the little fucking shit principal out. Tossing him in the back, I head towards the warehouse.

Dragging his piss and shit soaked body to the interrogation chair only makes me angrier. This little bitch can't even stand on his own two legs.

Slamming him down in the chair, I quickly secure his arms behind him. He's still screaming into the gag when I hear Lucifer walk into the room behind me.

"Has he said anything yet?" he asks me.

Shaking my head, I say, "Not yet. Just got him here."

Looking at the man's unsecured legs, he asks, "I'll call Harrold?"

"Probably for the best, Lucifer. I don't think this guy knows anything of use but he fucking ratted our daughters out."

Using medical scissors for his pant legs, I quickly have him stripped from his waist down. The little fuck is wailing again as I bring out the jumper cables.

Yanking the gag from his mouth, I say, "Tell me all you said, you little cockroach."

"Nothing! I didn't say a thing!"

"You told them where they were hiding!" I scream into his face.

Setting the jumper cable tips on each testicle, I watch his whole body lock up as he belts out an earsplitting scream. There are black scorch marks as I pull the tips off, then comes the smell of burning flesh.

The man screams again for a long time before I pull out a bottle of rubbing alcohol. "Here, let me make sure that doesn't get infected."

"Oh god, no!" he says as I pour it on his open wounds.

Shortly thereafter his eyes roll into the back of his head.

Dumping a bucket of water on his head brings him quickly back to consciousness. "You fat fuck! You told them where they were."

"I... I..."

"Shut the fuck up! Did you see any of the men that came in?"

Nodding his head, he goes into great detail of the men he saw charging into the school. And when he speaks of a man with almost white hair, I just about snip off the finger I've been taking chunks from.

Fucking dammit, I knew Ivan would be involved.

Putting my .45 to the principal's head, I give him a chance to say a final prayer. Pulling the trigger, I don't feel very happy about having let Ivan live right now.

This man's body in front of me is just the start of the many I expect to pile up before I get to Ivan.

I'm going tear him apart, limb from fucking limb.

20

AMY

Abigail is gone...

Gone.

I don't know how much time has passed since I was at the school and since Johnathan brought me home, but it's too much. It's been too long.

"Have you heard anything?" I ask Johnathan, desperate for any news when he walks into the living room from the kitchen.

His eyes drop to my wringing hands and then slowly slide back up to my face.

With a frown he shakes his head. "Not yet, but they're working on it."

He settles his big body on the couch and pulls out his phone.

I have the strongest urge to scream. To pick something up and fucking break it.

Instead, I pace in front of the TV. Now that the shock

has worn off and my head has cleared, I feel like I'm going crazy with inaction.

I need to do something. I need to get Abigail back. I just can't sit here, waiting for things to play out on their own.

Ivan has my little girl and I want to fucking kill him.

Ten more minutes pass. I pace and pace until Johnathan's phone rings. Whirling around on him, I watch him intently as he answers.

"Yeah?" he says into the phone.

I wish I could hear whatever is being said on the other end.

He grunts.

And grunts some more.

What a fucking Neanderthal!

"Okay," he finally says.

There's another grunt and he hangs up.

I stare at him. He seems completely oblivious to it.

"Well?" I snap, and tap my thigh impatiently. "Any news?"

His eyes jump up to me in surprise. "Not yet."

I throw my hands up in the air. I'm so frustrated I could fucking cry.

I stomp out of the living room and head into the kitchen to get away from Johnathan before I throw something at him.

Why would Ivan take Abigail? Why? The only reason I can think of is to get to me... But why go through all this trouble to do that?

I stop pacing and lean against the kitchen counter. Thinking.

When has anything Ivan's done in regards to me ever made sense? He's fucking obsessed with me and sick.

He could have taken Lucifer's daughter, he could have used her as a bargaining chip, but no, he took Abigail. Why?

Because he knows I'd do anything to get her back.

I can just sit here, waiting for the men to handle it. I trust Andrew, but I know Ivan. And knowing that Abigail is with him, unprotected...

Fuck. I need to contact him. I need a phone.

I don't think Johnathan will just give me his though if I ask for it.

Spinning around, my eyes scan the kitchen, looking for something to use to persuade Johnathan to let me use his phone.

Booze? No, that would take too long.

A knife? No, too messy...

A rolling stick? Not heavy enough.

I pick up the cast iron skillet, weighing it in my hand, then I swipe the dishes off the counter.

They crash to the floor.

"Amy? Are you okay?" Johnathan calls out, and I hear his heavy footsteps as he comes running to the kitchen to check on me.

When he appears in the doorway, I take a deep breath then swing the skillet at his head. It connects with his temple and the pan thrums in my hand.

Johnathan just stares at me, his eyes wide and confused.

"The fuck?" he slurs.

I swing at his head again and connect. This time he sways on his feet, his eyes rolling up as he collapses.

I jump back to avoid being taken down with him.

Opening my hand, I allow the skillet fall to the floor then I squat down and check him for a pulse. I find it in his neck. Steady and strong.

Good, I didn't accidentally kill him.

I check his pockets, pulling out his phone, keys, and wallet. Then I straighten and run out of the kitchen.

I run for the garage, figuring I should leave before Johnathan wakes up to stop me. I'll take his car, call Ivan and try to sweet talk Ivan into giving me back Abigail. I know from experience if I can placate Ivan even a little bit he usually forgives me for anything I've done.

I'm halfway to the Expedition when I remember Ivan's diamond necklace. Maybe if I wear it, I'll be able to better convince him...

Spinning on my heel, I run back into the house and up the stairs. I find the necklace right where I left it, under Abigail's pillow.

Running back downstairs, I'm panting heavy from rushing. Still, over the sound of my own heavy breathing, I can hear Johnathan groaning as he starts to come to in the kitchen.

Shit.

I run into the garage and hit the button for the door. I

only allow it to roll halfway up before I'm crawling under it.

I run to Expedition parked in the driveway, jump in and shift it into reverse.

Johnathan appears as the garage door slides up completely.

"Amy!" he bellows, and then clutches his head as if he's in pain. "Fuck! Stop!"

I jam the button to lock the doors then hit the gas. I squeal out of the driveway, fishtailing and nearly taking out the mailbox before I hit the brakes.

Johnathan comes running out of the garage and I yank the shifter into drive. He chases after me, waving his arms in the air and cursing.

But I don't stop. I can't stop.

Abigail needs me.

I drive like a madwoman. Ignoring stop signs and the speed limit.

I wait until I'm pulling out of the neighborhood before I dial Ivan. Punching his number into the phone, I hold my breath, and nearly jump out of my skin when the ringing comes through the speakers.

"Hello?" Ivan answers, sounding irritated.

"Ivan?" I say tentatively, unsure of his reaction.

"*Myshka*?" Ivan breathes in surprise. "Is that you?"

"Yes!" I choke out, relieved that he picked up. I don't know what I would have done if I couldn't get in touch with him.

"Where are you?" he asks. "Who are you with?"

"I don't know where I am," I answer him honestly.

None of the streets look familiar to me. I've never been on this side of the city before. This is a newer subdivision that looks like it just popped up. Everything is new —the disturbed dirt, the paint on the streets, and the traffic signs. There's even a little shopping center that matches the design of the houses.

"Who's with you?"

"No one. I got away. Someone—"

"Ah, little one, you did well. Do you have a GPS?"

"Yes. I'm pretty sure the phone does. Ivan, someone took—"

"Good. Good," Ivan purrs. "I'm going to give you an address. I want you to meet me at the address."

"Okay," I agree, a little frustrated he keeps cutting me off.

I pull into the parking lot of the shopping center.

Ivan rattles off an address and I punch it into the phone. The GPS gives me a route and an estimated arrival of fifteen minutes.

"Do you have it, *myshka*?"

"Yes, I think I know how to get there..."

"If you have any trouble, call me," he says firmly.

"I will," I state and then take a deep breath.

I know he has her, I know it, yet... what if he doesn't?

"Ivan," I exhale. "Someone took Abigail."

"I know."

I wait a moment, expecting him to say more. When he doesn't, I ask. "Did you?"

"We'll discuss it when you get here."

There's a little click and I stare at the display screen.

Is that it? Is that all he's going to say on the matter?! I push a couple of buttons but nothing happens.

The line dead, the car switches over to the radio. Heavy metal music starts blaring. I scream and pound my hands against the steering wheel.

That fucker, I know he has her. Why didn't he just say it?

I scream once more and then turn off the music.

Getting myself under control, I focus on the plan. I need to keep my shit together if we're going to make it through this.

I'm going to meet Ivan and convince him I've been held against my will so he won't hurt Abigail. He'll be angry, of course, but I've dealt with his anger before...

If I'm smart, he won't kill me, he'll just knock me around a bit.

With the plan in my head, I throw a glance over my shoulder and reverse out of the spot. The GPS starts spitting out directions to me once I'm back on the main road.

I'm five minutes into the drive when Johnathan's phone starts ringing. I almost answer it out of habit and glance at the screen.

The words—Andrew calling—nearly give me a heart attack.

I'm so not answering that.

The phone rings and rings. It stops for a moment only to start ringing again.

Shit.

Andrew tries to call three more times before the phone falls silent.

I can't talk to him; I can't give him the chance to stop me.

I'm going to get Abigail back.

I push the gas a little harder and check the rear-view mirror. It's not possible but I've got the strangest feeling that Andrew is somewhere behind me, following me.

I run through the next red light.

The phone starts ringing again. This time when I glance at the screen it reads—Lucifer calling.

Oh fuck no. I'm not stopping now.

I blow through the next two lights, narrowly avoiding an accident. Thankfully, I get lucky with the next light and then I'm turning onto the street where I'm supposed to meet Ivan.

The GPS leads me behind a strip mall. There's only one other car back here, parked beside the dumpster. I pull up and park beside it.

The car is a sleek, shiny black and the windows are so dark I can't see through them. I stare and stare, then suddenly remember I didn't put the necklace on. I'm scrambling to get it clasped behind my neck when there's a slight rapping on my window.

"Unlock the door," a muffled voice says.

I hesitate for only a second before hitting the button.

The lock pops up and my door is immediately pulled open. Before I can grab the phone a black-gloved hand reaches in and grabs my hands. My seatbelt is unsnapped and then I'm yanked out of the car.

I hit the pavement, dropping to my knees, and then I'm yanked back up. I'm half-dragged, half-pushed to the other car by two strange men clad in all black.

"Where's Ivan?" I ask frantically, afraid I've made a big mistake. Is this a trap?

"Don't worry, *myshka*, I'm right here," Ivan purrs from inside the car.

I'm shoved through the back door and nearly fall onto Ivan's lap.

The car door shuts behind me.

21

AMY

"Little one, how I've missed you," Ivan says huskily, grabbing me and pulling me closer to him.

I fight the urge to pull back, to stiffen, and will my body to relax.

I can do this. I can do this, I repeat inside my head.

I can endure anything to get Abigail back.

Ivan settles me on his lap and wraps an arm around my back, his hand coming to rest on my hip. His other hand tips my chin up, forcing me to look at him.

I stare at his face as his eyes roam over me possessively. He looks rougher than I remember. There's a strain around his eyes I don't recognize, and his nose is crooked, ruining his perfection.

"Where's Abigail?" I ask.

His phone starts ringing.

The car starts up and backs up. Then I sense us rolling forward.

Ivan's hand drops away, shoving into his pocket. He pulls out his phone and gives me that look he always gives me whenever he has to take a call.

"Hello?" Ivan answers, and then the rest of the conversation is in Russian.

His eyes drop to my chest, lingering on the little bit of cleavage I'm showing while he talks to whoever is on the line.

I wait and I wait. Squirming on top of his lap with impatience. Then I just can't wait any longer for him to finish.

"Where's Abigail?" I whisper. "Do you have her?"

He ignores me. The hand on my back drags up. He gathers up my hair and pulls it off my shoulders.

"Where's Abigail?" I repeat. I don't know how the fuck I'm going to convince him I don't hate his guts if he keeps ignoring me like this.

His hand comes around. His fingers tracing the curve of the necklace.

"Can I see her?"

His fingers follow the necklace until they near my cleavage. Then they break away to trace lightly against the tops of my breasts

"Ivan," I say, reaching up and grabbing his hand. "Please."

Something flashes in his eyes. Fuck. It's been so long I've forgot who I'm dealing with.

He snaps something sharp into the phone then lowers it to the seat.

"Yes," he says softly, menacingly. "I have her."

"Where is she? Can I see her?"

"Yes, you can see her after we arrive."

He starts to pick up his phone.

"Is she hurt?" I ask.

"No, she's not hurt," he answers impatiently, dropping the phone back down to the seat.

Before I can relax with relief, he grabs me by the chin and squeezes painfully.

I stare into his eyes and watch all his features tighten with anger.

"You know better than to interrupt my calls, *myshka*."

He waits for me to nod my head, to acknowledge it. I do know. I've learned this lesson before, painfully.

His thumb strokes across my bottom lip. My heart thumps sickly behind my ribs.

For a moment, I wonder if he's going to kiss me. To me that would be a punishment...

His thumb falls away and his fingers tighten around my cheeks.

His fingers squeeze and squeeze until I let go of his hand and cry out in pain.

"Now shut your mouth before I fuck it, Amy," he hisses.

I flinch, expecting him to hit me.

Fuck, this was such a bad idea. I've only been with him for a few minutes and I'm already pissing him off.

He smiles, his bright eyes glittering dangerously then he releases me. He picks his phone off the seat and mutters something in Russian. A moment later he laughs and I shrink away, knowing I just got off easy.

I spend the rest of the car ride looking out the window while his hand roams all over me. Chilling me until I feel nothing at all.

He has Abigail, I keep reminding myself. My fingers curl, my nails digging into my palms.

Outside the window, tall, familiar buildings scroll by. We drive deep into the city, then the scenery becomes less familiar as we enter a ghetto. It's like watching a future time lapse video sped up. The houses begin to rot from neglect, crumbling away before my eyes.

The street we turn down is more field than lawns. We pull up in front of an old, deteriorating Victorian mansion.

It looks like he's really come down in the world.

The door pops open and Ivan gives me a nudge, expecting me to get out.

I slide off his lap and out the door. The two men dressed in all black await me.

I try not to let them freak me out as I take in the outside of the house. It's quiet around here, there's not much going on, and I don't see any other guards. These two will have to sleep sometime. If I can find Abigail and slip out of the house, it may not be that hard to get away.

Ivan comes out of the car behind me and his hand

nudges the small of my back. I start forward, his hand guiding me up the steps of the house.

I await until we're inside the front hallway before I ask, "Where's Abigail?"

He doesn't answer. He leads me down the dark hallway and opens a door on the right.

"Can I see her?"

He shoves me inside.

Slamming the door behind him, we're thrust into the dark.

"Ivan?" I gasp, spinning around.

The light flickers on.

"*Myshka*," Ivan purrs while loosening his tie. "I've missed you."

I take a step back as he yanks off his tie. "I want to see my daughter."

Slowly Ivan shakes his head and begins to unbutton his cuffs. "After I'm done."

He takes a step forward and I take another step back, glancing behind me. We're in a bedroom. The curtains are all closed, and a large, king-sized bed is pushed up against the wall.

He takes another step forward and I take another step back, carefully avoiding the bed.

"Please," I plead. It feels like I've been doing a lot of this, pleading with him when I was expecting to manipulate him.

He closes the distance between us, backing me up against the wall. He looms over me, caging me in with his body, and then he strokes the back of his hand across my cheek.

Remembering that I wanted to use his feelings for me to give me what I want, I force myself to lean into his caress. To act like it doesn't make my skin crawl.

"I won't be able to relax until I see her," I murmur.

His hand stills and I glance up, hoping to see him softening towards me.

Instead, his eyes narrow to slits. Cold and hard.

Grabbing me by the back of my head, he yanks on my hair, forcing my chin up.

"Now you know how I felt," he says angrily, and then he's brutally kissing my mouth.

His lips smash mine against my teeth and his fingers tighten in my hair.

I reach up and try to push him away. He breaks the kiss and shoves me into the wall.

Panting heavily, he stares at me like he can't decide what to do. His eyes wavering between pleasure and pain.

Before I can think of something to say, a means to placate him in some way, he's grabbing me and kissing me again.

I start to taste blood before his tongue forces its way into my mouth.

"Amy," he groans as his tongue touches mine, tasting my blood.

He starts to relax against me and I fight the urge to bite the fucker off. Instead, I force myself to relax into the kiss.

"I've been so worried."

His hand covers my breast, cupping and squeezing me through my blouse.

His knees try to force their way between my knees and it's everything I can do to keep myself from kneeing him in the balls.

"I kept waiting for Lucifer to ransom you to me..."

As if just remembering something, he stiffens against me and pulls away. "Why didn't Lucifer ransom you to me?"

I don't know what to tell him. If I tell him about Andrew, he'll kill me and I'll never see Abigail.

None of this is working out the way I thought it would work out.

"Why didn't he ransom you to me?" he asks.

I open my mouth but nothing comes out.

"Did he touch you?" he asks angrily, his fingers squeezing around my breast.

"No!" I cry out and try to jerk away.

"Don't lie to me. Why else wouldn't he give you back to me?!"

I grab at his hand, my eyes watering with tears as I try to pull his hand off. He squeezes and squeezes until it hurts so much I'm sinking to my knees.

"Lucifer didn't touch me, Ivan... Please stop hurting me!" I beg when I fail to yank him off.

His fingers tighten and I scream. "He didn't!"

Then suddenly the pain stops.

"I believe you," he says.

I sob and slump against the wall.

"I'm sorry, *myshka*. I believe you," he says while reaching for me, his voice thick with remorse.

I shake my head and try to ward him off with my hands but he just knocks them away and drags me back up.

My breast throbs with pain and I can't stop sobbing.

Ivan kisses me like he's trying to apologize to me. It's sweet and tender at first but quickly turns vicious when I don't start to respond.

"I'm sorry," he says angrily, kissing me hard. "You drive me fucking crazy, Amy. The thought of another man touching what's mine..."

He kisses me harder, deeper. His tongue is like a worm in my mouth.

I shake my head and try to push him away. I can't do this, I can't.

I thought I could pretend to get us out of this but I hate him too fucking much.

"What more do you fucking want from me?" he asks, ripping his mouth away. "I said I was sorry, you ungrateful little bitch."

The question may be rhetorical and said in anger but it doesn't stop me from reminding him, "I want Abigail."

He stills and regards me silently. It's everything I can do to keep from shrinking beneath his gaze.

Then he suddenly reaches down and tries to yank my skirt up. "You'll get what you want after I get what I want."

"No!" I shriek and slap his hands away.

"You little bitch," he snarls and backhands me across the face.

Momentarily stunned, he manages to get my skirt up.

His fingers run along the crotch of my panties and suddenly I can move again. I kick, scream and punch at him, trying to fight him off. I get in a couple of blows to his chest and face before he captures my hands.

When he yanks my arms above my head, I bring my knee up, ramming it into his balls. He drops my arms and doubles over.

I slip around him and make a dash for a door. Running like my life depends upon it, I get my hand on the door knob before I'm yanked back and thrown to the floor.

"You fucking cunt! I gave you everything and this is how you repay me?" Ivan bellows, coming down on top of me.

"You're just like the rest of them. Taking and taking!" He reaches down and grabs the diamond necklace around my throat.

Twisting the necklace, he starts using the chain to choke me. "I'm tired of fucking giving! It's time to take what I want!"

22

ANDREW

Fuck. It's not Johnathan's fault that Amy got away, but I can't help wishing he had a thicker fucking skull.

As soon as he was able to get to a phone he called me, and thank the fucking devil himself I was so damn close to the house. Whatever Amy fucking thinks this will accomplish though is beyond me. Putting herself in jeopardy now will only put Abigail in further jeopardy.

Thank fuck for being able to track another person's phone. "Give me your password Johnathan."

"Fuck, capital J one tits."

"J one tits?" What the fuck?

"Yeah..."

"Alright, thanks."

Hanging up with him, I call Simon next. "Track Johnathan's phone."

Giving him the details on the phone, I wait as I hear

him typing into something. "Got it. You aren't too far from her. She's heading west on Old Mill road."

"Got it, now lock in on my phone and see if there's an opportunity to intercept her.".

There's too much silence right now, I need to try to reach her. "I have to try calling her. I'll call right back."

"Okay."

Dialing Amy five times is killing me. Each time she doesn't answer, I feel my heart sinking lower and lower. This is such a stupid fucking move on her part. I know she wants to protect Abigail, but we have to do this the right way or it all goes fucking wrong.

Not getting an answer, I call Simon back. "No answer."

"Okay, you should be able to get behind her at Old Mill and Harper," Simon says through the phone. "But you need to hurry."

Pushing the pedal down to the floor, I fly through a couple of greenlights. Thank fuck something is going my way today. My daughter kidnapped... that stupid fucking principal... Paul dying.

This fucking day is one I would happily remove from memory.

Ahead of me, I see a long line of red tail lights stopped at a red light. Shit. Coming to a slow halt in the Mercedes, Simon bursts through the line. "She just went through the intersection. You need to hurry up."

"Fuck!" Slamming the pedal back down while whipping the wheel to the left, I start racing up the wrong side of the yellow line. My hands slip the wheel again as I come to the red light in the intersection.

I slam on the breaks, and a car narrowly missing my nose as I take a fast left.

"You need to hurry up, she just turned into a shopping center."

"Shit, I bet it's a meet up. Probably called Ivan."

"That would be my first guess since she has made only one call since taking Johnathan's phone."

"Can you track the phone?" I ask as I try pushing through another intersection but the traffic has me dead in my tracks.

I'm completely unable to find a lane to slip in.

"I already have, it's in a car waiting in the shopping center."

Fuck, that's good.

"Okay, where's my turn off?"

"Andrew, hear me out on something."

"Simon..." I growl in warning. I have no time or desire to play a single fucking game right now.

"Follow them, Andrew. It's a safer bet on getting Abigail back without as much trouble than if you go in right now, guns blazing. They might be able to get away, and then we're at square one again."

Sweat breaks out on my forehead as I move the car to the left and squeeze past an old lady who rightly gives me the middle finger.

Pushing the pedal back down, the large motor roars as I move through the intersection.

"Andrew, think about…"

"Shut the fuck up!" I yell. "I'll do it, just fucking shut up."

The line goes silent as I slow the car down. It takes all my control not to push the pedal down. To not race after Amy.

"You want me to do this for the intel don't you?" I ask between clenched teeth.

"Of course, but it's also the best strategy we currently have. I don't have a team in your area of town. The closest right now is thirty minutes out."

"I'm not going to back off of them, Simon."

"I know. Pull up into the parking lot directly across from the shopping center, it should have a pizza place. Park there to get a good view of who exits and leaves."

Taking a right into the parking lot, I back into a slot next to a minivan.

I don't have to wait long though before Simon urgently says, "Move now, the car's taking a right out of the shopping center."

Shit. There are three cars pulling out but only one has the look that I'm willing to bet my life on. Tinted windows on a new Lincoln. From what I can see, there are two men in the front but I'm not sure about the back.

Following them in my car isn't too hard. They aren't fleeing the area and the traffic is heavy enough that I can be easily confused as just another motorist.

Questions and questions float through my mind as I try to figure out what the fuck happened with Ivan. How the fuck did he get past our noses? How the fuck did he get back into the country?

He shouldn't have been able to with the no-fly Simon had slapped on him.

Fuck. None of this makes any fucking sense. Especially when I think of how he figured out where Abigail would be at. That's worrying me.

How the fuck do we do anything right now? Was he watching the school after the first strike team was taken out? What the hell does he know? Motherfucker is going to fucking die, I swear.

I'm going to beat him with my own fucking hands.

"Simon," I say as I fall even further back. We're getting out of the busy areas and slowly moving through the less crowded areas of town.

"Fall back a mile or so. I've got them so far, he's on a phone call. As long as he doesn't shut his phone off completely, we'll be good."

Easing my foot off the pedal, I try to tell myself that charging in isn't the way to handle things. I know in my head it isn't.

But my Amy is in that fucking car, and my Abigail is fucking... somewhere.

The dark sky is as clear as I've ever seen it in the last two shitty months. The moon nowhere to be seen. It's going to get cold tonight, no cloud cover for us.

"They've pulled into a house on your left-hand side. Two miles ahead of current position. I would suggest you do not proceed until we have a team there. We're twenty minutes out."

"Fuck you, Simon," I say with a smile. "Tell the boys I'll leave the lights on for 'em."

Pushing disconnect on the phone, I toss it to the passenger seat.

I drive past the house for half a mile before finding a side road. Dumping my car into a culvert, I quickly grab the weapons I have in the car. Two .45's with silencers, full clips.

It's not much but from the lack of presence at the house I passed, I don't really see needing more than what I got.

It's a quick jog from where I left the car to the house, and during that time I've got a plan slowly formulating in my head. It's one of two choices—I go in guns blazing or I try to be stealthy about the whole thing.

Finding no sentries in the field around the house surprises me somewhat, but not really. They're cocky that they got Abigail and Amy without being caught.

The first guy I come across is lazily leaning against the black Lincoln I saw earlier. It's one of two cars in the long curved driveway.

Moving up to his side quickly, I slap a hand over his mouth as I put the barrel of my gun to the side of his head.

We both stand still as statues before my lips finally get close to his ear.

I murmur quietly, "How many in the house if you want to live..."

He shakes his head and I can tell he doesn't want to talk, stupid fuck. Pulling the trigger slightly, I say, "Okay, I'll ask the next guy."

Just like I thought, he starts talking behind my hand.

Pulling the hand slowly away, I say, "Be quiet. How many in the house?"

"Three. Two guys and the boss."

"Where are they in the house?"

"Two in the front room, boss in the back room with the girl. Upstairs is the little one."

"Thanks."

Pulling the trigger, I hear blood explode loudly out the side of his head.

I lied. Fuck him.

Going to the front of the house, I try to walk as casually as I can. Very gently, I test the front door handle.

It's unlocked.

I have to shake my head at the whole situation now. It's damn typical of how things are in real life. People just don't prepare themselves like they do in the movies.

Opening the door, I poke my head in.

In the living room I see the back of two guy's heads lounging on the couch. They've got their eyes focused on some shitty action movie. If I didn't have to kill them I would have suggested they take notes on how bad guys protect themselves.

Walking around the couch, I would say something

witty but... fuck that. The last thing they see is me stepping in front of them, lifting both pistols in the air.

Firing with both hands, I put holes through their chests then their heads.

Three men down, one to go.

A loud scream floats down the halls from the back of the house and rips my heart from my chest.

It's Amy.

I can hear her pain. I can hear the bellows of a man I can only assume is Ivan as I slowly make my way past the staircase.

Heading down the long hall, towards the back of the house, I try to make sure every room is clear. It won't do to finally get my hands on the bastard only to have some Russian cock-smoker shoot me in the back.

When I finally get to the door, I hear a gurgling sound coming through it.

Leaning back, I lift my leg and kick the door right next to the handle as hard as I can.

Watching the door fly inward, I get my first view of Ivan. He's looming over Amy, his hands wrapped tightly in the chain that is choking her throat.

He's going to kill her and my unborn child.

Throwing myself across the room, I slam into his arms with all I have in me. It's good that I surprised the asshole because his hands come flying free of Amy as we go tumbling over a bed and into a nightstand.

There's a loud crack of wood and we drop to the floor like a sack of fucked up potatoes.

I roar in rage as he throws me off of him.

Rolling to a crouch, I back away from him. Straightening back up to my full height, I look to Amy. She's there, kneeling on the floor, gasping for air. Her hands are at her neck, tearing at the necklace that dug into her throat.

Looking back to Ivan, I grin when he fumbles standing up. He tries to go for the door of the room only to have me catch him, my foot sticking between his legs.

Falling to the floor, I push him to his back. He looks up at me with fear as I grin at him.

"You touched my wife, Ivan... You tried to hurt my wife and unborn child," I say quietly.

"How dare you touch her!" he yells up at me, but from my position he looks like a little bitch.

He tries to stand but I kick out his legs again.

Plopping down on his back, he isn't too far from Amy. His voice is almost soft as he looks to her. "How could you let him?"

She doesn't talk to him. Her eyes are weeping as she continues to cough, trying to catch her breath.

The breath he could have stolen from her forever.

"How'd you find Abigail, asshole?" I ask as I land a kick to his ribs.

Coughing out loud, he says, "Fuck you!"

"Not the answer I'm looking for, asshole."

A second kick to his ribs has him wheezing. "We saw her when... you put her in there... you think we quit watching his kids?"

"So this was another sanctioned hit then?"

He actually starts laughing. The crazy fuck is laughing at me. "No, asshole. This was my thing."

"So why the fuck are you laughing, dickless?"

He's quiet as he stares deep into my eyes. Then he says, "I'll wait until your boss comes to question me again."

"Not going to happen, Ivan. You'll be dead long before they get here."

"Bullshit! I'm too valuable, you fucking peasant!"

"Why the laughter then?"

"Because something's happening and they won't even tell me, their biggest backer, about it! You fools. I'll be your only chance of living... Give me the bitch and I will find out all that I can."

Dropping down on top of him, my first punch lands in the middle of his nose. The loud crunch breaks through Amy's sobs and his loud scream.

Straddling his chest, I swing down with a second punch. This one lands on the side of his flapping mouth.

There's another loud crack and I feel his jaw breaking.

"She's mine," I shout into his face.

From there, my fists are the only thing I think of, the only things connecting me to this world.

One after the other they punch his face.

Somewhere after the fifth or six punch, I feel my knuckle break. It snaps almost as loud as his nose did.

Screaming out in anger, I hit him with the opposite hand before leaning back.

He's not moving or making any noise now.

I guess he passed out.

Pushing the thumb of my good hand into his eye socket, I hear his eyeball pop right before he wakes up, screaming through a mangled face. He's a blubbering mess now.

I highly doubt he even knows why he's hurting.

Looking to my left, I see Amy staring at me. She isn't sobbing anymore, only watching me with wide, unjudging eyes.

My throat must be pretty raw because as I speak I realize I have been roaring at the pile of shit the whole time.

"Are you okay, baby?" I ask softly.

Her head bobs up and down briefly before she says, "Yes."

"You want to get in on this before he dies?"

A quick shake of her head is the only answer I get.

"He's going to die now. I can't allow anyone to ever come between us."

"I... I know," she says as she nods to me.

Staring into her eyes, I feel my hands wrapping tightly around Ivan's throat.

Squeezing, my broken knuckle aches with misery.

It's okay though, I only have to kill him now. I can live through this pain.

Amy doesn't look away from me as I kill Ivan. She

watches as I strangle the very life from him, staring into my eyes.

Still, I see no judgment.

And I feel this strange spark inside of me.

When Ivan's body no longer moves, I slowly stand up from him.

Walking over to Amy, I reach down and take her hand in mine then pull her up to me.

Somewhere along the way to this house, I realized how much she means to me. She's more than just a possession. She's not property to me... she's my other half. She's my soul completed.

Will words be enough to get her to understand how much I care for her? I have no clue. I don't think she has ever understood the lengths I would go to keep her by my side.

Love.

Fuck me. It's fucking love.

Walking out of the bedroom, I pull Amy behind me. Her small, delicate hand is so warm inside my own. Shit, it still hurts to move the fucking knuckle though.

Pulling her with the broken hand and leading with the other holding a gun, we walk up the stairs carefully.

Poking our heads in each room, we don't find Abigail until we get to the master bathroom. She's quietly hiding in the bathtub, her little hands over her ears.

"Abigail, my heart!" Amy all but wails as she pulls the frightened girl into her arms.

Wrapping my arms around both of my girls, I squeeze them as hard as I can.

The loves of my life both safe and in my protection once again.

I swear though I will never let them go again.

~

SIMON IS PACING in front of Lucifer and I as he goes through a litany of curse words. They range from how much of a Neanderthal I am, to the doubting of my parents being more than female dogs.

He's as pissed as I have ever seen him.

He's so mad right now he's actually sweating. His tie is pulled off and the suit jacket he was wearing has been thrown in a corner of the office.

"How could you possibly kill him, Andrew!" he spits out as he stares me down.

"He hurt Amy, and I questioned him before he died. No reason not to."

"Ivan could have been a bargaining chip for us!"

Looking to Lucifer, I shrug my shoulders. "I didn't see a reason in letting him have a chance to get loose again."

"That's not your decision!" Simon yells.

Lucifer shrugs. "He was...onsite, Simon, we were not."

Knowing I have Lucifer's backing in this, I turn back to Simon. "He said something big was happening, but even he didn't know what. Don't you think you should be figuring that out?"

258 | IZZY SWEET & SEAN MORIARTY

Turning away from them both, I carefully put my raincoat on over my suit.

It's cold and rainy as fuck yet again.

My hand throbbing, I look back to them both. "I'm going home to my girls, Simon. Ivan said this was his own job. I think he was telling the truth; just like I think there's something bigger in the works."

Walking out of the fucker's office, I leave the door open, debating if I should go back in there and throttle the bastard.

Ivan was dead as soon as he took Abigail. What the fuck did he expect me to do? Sit back? Fuck that shit.

No one touches what's mine.

EPILOGUE

Amy

Two months later

Standing in front of Andrew, holding his hand as I state my vows, I feel every word I say in the very depths of my soul.

"I, Amy Johnson, take thee Andrew Baxter for my lawful husband..."

I stare deep into his dark eyes and I feel so much love. So much hope.

He's everything I want. Everything I'll ever need.

"To have and to hold, from this day forward..."

After all we've been through the future looks so bright.

"For better, for worse..."

I remember that day, not too long ago, when he killed a man for me...

"For richer, for poorer..."

When he strangled Ivan's life out of him with his bare hands while staring me in the eyes. There was so much love there, so much love...

"In sickness and in health..."

He's killed for me. He's killed for Abigail. He did for me what I couldn't do for myself.

If that isn't love, I don't know what is.

"Until death do us part," I finish and Andrew smirks like he's in on some secret joke.

I blink up at him, not understanding his amusement. He squeezes my hand and glances towards the priest.

The priest acknowledges our consent and then declares, "What God joins together, let no one put asunder."

Our rings are blessed and then we exchange them. As I repeat after the priest and slide my ring over his finger, I marvel at all the scars on his knuckles.

He's lead such a violent, brutal life...

He slides his ring over my finger and I look back up at him.

I know who he is and I know what he is. And I accept him. I know without a doubt he will always protect us, his family.

There's another blessing and a prayer but staring up at Andrew, it's hard to pay attention to anything but him.

Finally, the priest announces, "You may kiss your bride!"

Andrew sweeps me up into his arms and gives me a very deep, very sinful kiss in front of the congregation.

Cheers erupt around us. I hear Abigail and Evie squealing with joy.

The music starts up and I feel like I'm in daze.

Andrew leads me down the aisle and we step outside the church to shake hands and receive our congratulations.

The sun beams down on us as we stand on top of the steps and the day is so wonderful, so glorious, I foolishly feel like nothing could possibly ruin it.

This is the happiest day of my life.

Lily, my maid of honor, and my other bridesmaids gather around me as Andrew and Lucifer thank the last of the guests for attending. Andrew is shaking hands with the mayor of Garden City and inviting him to the reception when a child suddenly cries out.

Everyone turns to see what happened.

A little boy I don't recognize, who can't be more than five or six, sits on the bottom step, crying.

Lily and I rush over to help him. His mother reaches him first and squats down beside him, pulling him into her arms. She rocks and murmurs to her son until he quiets down.

Then she points an accusing finger at Adam.

"That little monster just pushed my Mason down the stairs."

Lily gasps with indignation. "He wouldn't."

Lily and I turn towards the children while Lucifer approaches the woman, soothing her with an apology and a hand up.

Adam stands beside Abigail, his chin up in the air and his young eyes full of defiance. Lily looks at the little boy then back at Adam

"Adam?" Lily starts then thinks better of it. She presses her lips together and watches the woman walk off with her son before saying more.

I dismiss the rest of the bridesmaids, sending them off to the reception without me.

Once the woman and Mason are out of sight and Lucifer returns, Lily asks Adam, "Did you push that little boy down the stairs?"

Adam looks his mother dead in the eye and shows no remorse. "Yes."

We both gasp and I feel Andrew joining my side. His hand covers my hand and his fingers squeeze mine.

The color draining from her face, Lily shakes her head in disbelief. "Why? Why would you do that?"

"Because he's protecting what's his," Lucifer says as he comes up the steps.

"What do you mean, 'what's his'?" Lily asks shrilly, dividing her attention now between her husband and son.

"He was trying to kiss Abigail," Adam says stiffly and that's when I notice he and Abigail are holding hands. "I put a stop to it."

"So you pushed him down the stairs?" Lily repeats in disbelief.

Adam nods his head and his lips begin to turn up with just the hint of a smile. "Yes. It was the most effective way to get rid of him."

We all stare at him in shocked silence. Well, all of us except for one person...

Lucifer takes one look at us and laughs.

With pride, he walks over to Adam and then gives him a pat on the back.

And I'm filled with the most foreboding sense of dread when he says, "Like father, like son..."

THE END

PLAYLISTS

Available on Spotify

Amy's Playlist - http://spoti.fi/2rBXYMN

In The Air Tonight - Natalie Taylor
Call Me Devil - Friends in Tokyo
The Wolf - Phildel
Bad Dream - Ruelle
(I Just) Died in Your Arms - Epic Trailer version - Hidden Citizens
Real Life - Stealth
Burn - In This Moment
Kiss Me A Thousand Times - RAIGN
Oh Lord - In This Moment
All The King's Men - The Rigs
Still Running - Epic Trailer version - Hidden Citizens

Holding Out For A Hero - Nothing but Thieves

Andrew's Playlist - http://spoti.fi/2sjr007

Silence Speaks - While She Sleeps
Hooked - Fit For a King
Hurricane - Thrice
King of Mercy - Nine Shrines
B.M.F - Upon a Burning Body
Refuge - Northlane, In Hearts Wake
Eternally Yours - Motionless in White
Unbreakable - Of Mice & Men
War Is Killing Us All - Righteous Vendetta

ALSO BY IZZY AND SEAN

Disciples

Keeping Lily (Lucifer & Lily)

Stealing Amy (Andrew & Amy)

The Pounding Hearts Series

Banging Reaper (Chase & Avery)

Slamming Demon (Brett & Mandy)

Bucking Bear (Max & Grace)

Breaking Beast (Alexander and Christy)

By Sean Moriarty

Gettin' Lucky

Gettin' Dirty

By Izzy Sweet

Letting Him In

Stepbrother Catfish

ABOUT US

Izzy Sweet & Sara Page – The one and the same brain.

Sean Moriarty- The real life alpha bad boy that Izzy tamed.

Residing in Cincinnati, Ohio, Izzy and Sean are high school sweethearts that just celebrated their 10th wedding anniversary, though they've been together since they were teenagers – over fifteen years.

Both avid and voracious readers, they share a great love and appreciation for a great story, and attribute their early role-playing days as the fledgling beginnings of their joint writing career.

You can see more of our works at our website -
www.dirtynothings.com

KEEPING LILY

My husband traded me away to save his own life...

And now I belong to the devil.

One night and everything in my life changed. Two words and my world turned dark.

"Take her."

Owing the most ruthless crime lord in Garden City five million dollars, my husband chose to trade me and my children away to save himself.

I was on the cusp of freedom, so close to divorcing that scumbag I was married to.

Now I'm enslaved to a man who is obsessed with me. A man so wicked and beautiful they call him Lucifer.

So alluring, he makes the angels weep with envy. He's so powerful, I can't stop myself from bending to his will.

He's determined to master me, and he won't rest until I give him all.

He wants my light, and he wants my dark.

He wants my body, and he wants my heart.

But most of all, he wants the one thing I can't give him. The one thing I can't bear to part with...

My soul.

Chapter One

Lucifer

"Motherfucker!" Comes out of my mouth in a growl as I shake my hand.

The punch to this piece of shit's jaw sent tingling sensations up my arm.

Mickey Dalton sputters gibberish out of his busted lips. "I... I... Swear I will pay... just gotta..."

I'm tempted to keep this up, but fuck it. I have bigger fish to fry than this small time fucking gambler.

Looking over the man's shoulder, I nod to Andrew. "Ensure he fully understands how much he owes. Remove his pinky."

"Yes, sir." Andrew nods.

"Wha... No!" Mickey shouts as Andrew heads to the table where he keeps a black bag stowed.

Turning around, I look at Simon, my right-hand man. "Where are we at with the other three files?"

"Two have been collected on, the last I was waiting on your judgment."

"Marshall Dawson."

"He has flat out refused to cooperate with any of our attempts to collect. He believes his status is untouchable. He will give us no answer on where he was or what has happened to our money."

"Is he finally home?" I ask.

"Arrived earlier tonight."

A metallic snip rings out into the room followed by a high-pitched scream. I turn to see Andrew wiping the blood on the guy's t-shirt.

Andrew raises his voice only slightly as he grabs the man by the throat. "Stop fucking squealing, asshole. Lucifer doesn't like hearing pigs fucking about."

Walking out through the door and into the hall, I look to Simon. "How are the spreadsheets with Bart coming along?"

"Clean, with everything accounted for..."

"Yet, you still have doubts?" I ask him as we walk.

"I do. I just can't explain why."

"Keep an eye on him then."

SIMON HOLDS an umbrella over my head as we walk out of the abandoned hotel. The shattered glass door slams shut behind us as he ushers me into the sleek black Mercedes SUV.

Getting comfortable in the backseat, I reach over and pull the file left on the other seat for me. The name Marshall Dawson is neatly typed on the tab.

I let out a quiet sigh to myself. I knew this one was going to come back as a thorn in my side.

Marshall Dawson is a waste of breathable air. The man used the connections he had with my father and another city boss to secure a loan from us. Five million in *cash*.

Five fucking million dollars with nothing to show for it.

Five fucking million dollars down the drain.

I took this on as a favor to Sean O'Riley. A favor to a now dead and buried man.

Shit like that doesn't sit well with me. But when I went to the top to seek retribution, I was stonewalled. I was told the man who killed Sean, and all the surrounding issues, have been dealt with.

Fuck that. I want my pound of flesh.

Shaking my head, I open the file. It's no use going down that train of thought right now. I can pursue it another time if I need to.

I slowly flip through the pages we have on Marshall.

It's funny how we can put a file together on a person where he is reduced to twenty or so pages. I can see every payment he has made on his mortgage to how many times he has been in the overdraft with his bank.

I look at his legal outstanding debts, and I look at the five-million-dollar debt he now owes to me personally. Anger is slowly creeping through my veins.

Flipping through the pages, I look at his family life. Since he borrowed the money I have had one of my men keeping close tabs on his family. He is married to Lilith Merriweather, aged twenty-seven, and has two children, a boy and a girl. Both children under the age of seven.

I look at the picture of Marshall for a long time as we drive through the late-night rain. The man is closer to my father's age than mine. How did he marry a woman so young? Money and his slimy charm must have played a large part of it.

I look through the pictures of his family quickly. The children are pretty in a child way. Blonde hair and blue eyes, they must take after their mother. Marshall must have married way out of his league.

My fingers stop as the picture of his wife comes up. Emerald green eyes, sensuous pink lips, high cheek-bones, pale flawless skin and long blonde hair. All of those parts on their own would make her remarkable.

Even if her face was overall plain just one of her features would stun a person. But together they make something otherworldly.

She is beauty incarnate.

Fingers tracing the lines of her lips, I frown. How the hell did that man marry a woman like this? I flip further through the pictures of her. There aren't many, but what I do see shows me that she is unlike any other woman I have ever laid eyes on.

She is perfection.

There is a rather candid photo of her putting groceries in the back of her red Volvo station wagon. Her hair is all over the place. Her slender legs are encased in yoga pants, feet in Uggs. Her daughter looks like she is giving her problems as she tries to watch her and still put groceries in the back.

Even this... domesticity calls to me.

There is a glamour shot of some type mixed in and I can see just how haunting those eyes are. They are calling to me, pulling me in to get forever lost. I can feel my hands curling into themselves. She is pulling me from where I sit in the SUV.

"Take me to Marshall's, James," I say to my driver.

Looking back at me from the front seat, Simon says, "Now? You don't want to wait until tomorrow?"

"No. We're going there *now*."

The car makes a few turns as we pull off the freeway and then back on again.

My eyes drift out the window for a moment to look at the rain that has been pelting down on the city all week.

Looking back to the picture, though, I see something I haven't seen before—a light. Inside I feel an ember flaring to life.

My muscles are going taut with expectation.

I need to see this woman; I need to see if what the pictures show me is true.

Lily

MY HUSBAND, MARSHALL, is sleeping beside me, snoring loudly, and I have the strongest urge to smack him.

I want to scream in his pale, pudgy face. I want to tell him to wake the fuck up. I want to ask him why he's back in my bed.

But I just lay beside him and stare up at the ceiling instead.

It's time to accept reality.

Our marriage is done.

Dead.

Today was the final nail in the coffin.

First thing in the morning, after I get the kids off to school, I'm going to meet with a divorce attorney. I can't go on like this. This is no way to live, this is just...existing.

And I'm sick of it.

After growing up dirt poor, I married Marshall thinking I would finally have financial security. I would always have a roof over my head. I would never go hungry again.

Foolishly, I believed his lust for me would turn to love. That like an arranged marriage, our feelings for each other would grow after time. If we had children, we could make a real go of it.

But this, the lack of love, the lack of care, isn't worth it. I rather starve than stay in this loveless marriage.

Marshall has been gone for weeks, *traveling on business*. He's gone more than he's home. Ever since our first child, Adam, was born six years ago, he's been finding more and more reasons to leave us.

There's always some client on the other coast that needs his help. Or some corporation up north that has to have his expertise or they're going to lose millions on... something...

It's funny, even after almost eight years of marriage I still don't know exactly what his job title or true profession is. Whenever I ask him about it he just brushes me off, doesn't have time to explain it, or says I wouldn't understand.

Like I'm some kind of idiot.

If I was an idiot I wouldn't know about all the women he's been hooking up with. I know that's one of the reasons he's always leaving us. He has a girlfriend in every city.

Yet, he won't even touch me when I throw myself at him.

I sigh, looking down at the red nightie I bought from

Victoria's Secret and pull the blanket up to cover my breasts.

He won't even touch me when I've taken great pains to dress up for him.

Suddenly my eyes feel swollen and my nose stings. I have to blink back my tears and take a deep breath. Rolling my eyes back up, I focus on the ceiling.

This shouldn't hurt, dammit. This isn't a bad thing, this is good.

This is... *freedom*.

I no longer have to pretend this is a real marriage. No more keeping up appearances on Facebook. No more making excuses for him with my family and friends.

No more trying to explain to the children that daddy is sorry but he had to miss their birthday—again.

This is a fresh start, a new beginning.

I've been doing everything on my own for years now. Losing him won't make much of a difference.

Marshall suddenly grunts loudly and rolls over.

The air turns sour and I resist the urge to gag.

Gah, he is such a pig.

Chapter Two

Lily

I'm not sure what wakes me up. It could have been the light turning on.

Marshall's loud, "What the fuck?"

Or the soft, menacing voice that says, "Hello, Marshall. I'm not interrupting anything, am I?"

Even under my warm blanket, that voice sends a chill down my spine and I peel my eyes open, shivering.

At first, the light is too harsh on my eyes and I have to blink several times before the strange man standing in our bedroom comes into focus.

This must be a dream, I convince myself and squeeze my eyes shut. I open them again but I still just can't believe it.

There's no way that man is real.

Standing in the center of my bedroom, the man is illuminated by a halo of light coming from the lamp. The light seems to love him, clinging to him. He's glowing and so alluring, he looks almost angelic.

"What the fuck are you doing in my house? You can't just come walking in here..." Marshall sputters. His fat fists grab the blanket, yanking it away from me as he pulls it up his hairy chest.

I gasp as the cool air hits my breasts and the sound draws the attention of the angelic stranger. He turns his icy blue gaze on me and I'm utterly stunned as our eyes meet.

With just a look I feel held by him.

Trapped.

Frozen.

Helpless.

He's so beautiful it *hurts* to look upon him. The kind

of beauty that's so strong, so deeply felt, it's like experiencing a piece of music that *moves* you and staring into the sun at the same time.

Tears prick my eyes and my skin tingles as I break out in gooseflesh.

His face is a composition of features so perfect that now that I've glimpsed them I fear all other men will be forever compared to him.

Chiseled cheeks, full, pink lips. A strong jaw and straight nose. Blonde hair so pale it's nearly snow white and brushed back from his forehead.

It feels like an eternity passes as we stare at each other across my bedroom and then his eyes break away only to slide down, warming as they lock on the pale swells of my breasts.

A flush creeps up my chest. I'm not naked but in this little lacy nightie, I feel like I am.

I grab the blanket and Marshall cries out as I yank it back. He shoots me a dirty look but I give him my coldest glare and practically dare him to try and take it back.

Screw him, no one cares about his hairy man-chest.

The stranger watches our little tug of war, his lips curving with a hint of amusement.

Marshall finally gives up on trying to wrestle the blanket away from me and decides to steal my pillow instead. Covering his chest with my pillow, he hugs it tightly and puffs up as he says, "If you leave now, Lucifer, I'll forget this incident ever happened."

Lucifer? Is that the stranger's name? How strange and

morbid. Yet, I swear I've heard that name before, on the news or in the paper...

The stranger's eyes flash and the amusement disappears from his lips. Two dark shadows shimmer behind him and I swallow back a gasp as I realize those two shadows are two other men.

What the hell is going on? Who are these men and why are they in my bedroom? I turn to Marshall and watch him squirm uneasily.

What did Marshall do?

"You'll forget this ever happened?" Lucifer says coolly and his eyes narrow with menace. "Just like you forgot to pay me back the five million dollars you owe me?"

All the color drains instantly from Marshall's face and his eyes dart from side to side as if he's trying to figure out an escape plan. "I already paid that back. You'll have to talk to Sean if you want your money."

"Sean's dead."

I watch Marshall's mouth open then close, then open again. He sputters and gasps like a fish out of water, his face starting to turn blue from the lack of oxygen.

I can't believe Marshall borrowed five million dollars. What would he need with so much money? I know I haven't seen a penny of it.

"I paid Sean the money," Marshall finally gets out, and then rushes on to say, "I don't have five million to pay you..."

Lucifer takes a step towards our bed. "That's too bad."

"Wait!" Marshall cries out in panic, the grip of his

fingers tearing at the pillow he holds to his chest. "Maybe we can work something out? I could—"

"I've had a look at your assets. You have no means to pay me back," Lucifer says dismissively and takes another step toward the bed.

I look between Lucifer and Marshall and now I'm starting to feel panicked. Lucifer has only taken two steps towards our bed but there's clear menace in the way he's moving.

What is he going to do? Are they going to hurt Marshall?

Are they going to hurt me?

Lucifer takes another step and Marshall whimpers. He *whimpers*.

The sound has my hackles rising and I wonder if there's something I could do. I glance towards my phone on my nightstand. The moment I don't think they're looking at me I'm going to make a grab for it.

But it might be too late for Marshall by then...

I could start screaming, but the only good that will probably do is wake the children.

Marshall is pushing back against the headboard like he believes he could escape through the wall if he tries hard enough. Then he shoots a pleading look towards me.

As if I could help him...

Marshall's eyes widen suddenly as if he's had a revelation.

"You want my life as payment?" he squeaks out.

Lucifer lifts an eyebrow and inclines his head. "Yes. That's how these things usually go, isn't it?"

Marshall licks his lips nervously, looks to me then back to Lucifer. "Would you accept another life as payment?"

He's not about to say what I think he is, is he? No, he wouldn't. No decent human being...

Lucifer's upper lip curls with disdain but his voice sounds interested. "What are you proposing?"

Marshall is too cowardly to stop hugging his pillow so he nods his head to me instead. "Take her. Take my wife in my place."

I'm so shocked, so floored, I suck in a sharp breath that never ends.

"You want me to kill your wife?" Lucifer asks and it feels like all the warmth was just sucked out of the room.

"No, of course not..." Marshall recoils at the murderous look on Lucifer's face. "Just hold her as a deposit, an insurance, while I get you the five million."

"You mean a ransom?" Lucifer clarifies.

Marshall nods his head up and down. "Yes, yes, that's it. A ransom."

My lungs full of air, I expel it all in a loud, "How could you!" and make a lunge for Marshall.

I'm not an object he owns. He can't just trade me away to some creepy, beautiful stranger to save his own neck.

Marshall squeaks and scrambles away from me. I end up chasing him until he falls out of bed, landing on his ass.

I grip the edge of the mattress, panting with anger as I watch him scuttle backward until he bumps into Lucifer's legs.

"As much as I would love to accept your offer," Lucifer says as he pushes Marshall away with the toe of his shoe. "I'm afraid your wife is not worth the five million you owe me."

Damn. I blink up at Lucifer, feeling utterly conflicted. On one hand, I don't want to be given away, but on the other, it stings the ego a bit to hear I'm not worth five million dollars.

I snort though as Marshall goes to his hands and knees, kneeling in front of Lucifer to beg for mercy.

"Please," Marshall begs, reaching out and grabbing Lucifer's leg.

I'd pity him and try to help the poor bastard if he didn't just try to trade me away in his place.

"There has to be something else I can give you..." Marshall sobs.

Lucifer makes a face of disgust and looks down at Marshall like he's a bug he'd like to step on.

"Anything," Marshall wails as Lucifer kicks at him. "Anything."

I sit back on my heels and watch Marshall beg while taking the kick, wondering how all of this happened.

Lucifer's head lifts and his eyes lock on me. His features are still, utterly calm, but there's something dark stirring in the depths of his icy irises.

"Anything?" Lucifer queries.

"Yes, anything!" Marshall nods his head with sudden enthusiasm.

"I'll accept your offer," Lucifer grins at me. "If you give her to me permanently, and throw in your children."

"No, no! You can't!" I scream and I'm off the bed in an instant.

Marshall yelps and scuttles back until he's hiding behind Lucifer's legs.

Lucifer between us, blocking me, my hands clench into fists and I pant, trying to control the rush of rage that has flooded my head. I swear if Marshall offers this... this... inhuman monster my children, I'll strangle him with my bare hands.

Lucifer smirks down at me as if he finds all of this amusing. I bristle under that smirk but suddenly feel self-conscious standing so close to him. He's tall, with at least a foot on me, and I feel puny now standing in front of him.

"Well? Do we have a deal, Marshall?"

Marshall continues to use Lucifer as a shield like the coward he is. He pokes his head out only long enough to peek at me. "Yes!"

"No!" I screech and lunge forward, reaching around Lucifer to grab Marshall.

Marshall squeaks and stumbles backward, just out of my reach.

Lucifer grabs me by the arms, stopping my forward lunge and hauls me back. Chuckling, he pins my arms to my sides and I screech and struggle, trying to escape his grasp.

"We're done here, Marshall. I suggest you leave now before I change my mind..."

"Leave? Why do I have to leave? This is my house!" Marshall protests.

Head tipping back, I glare up at Lucifer and continue to struggle. Damn, he's stronger than he looks, though it is hard to tell just how built he is under that suit he's wearing.

Once again Lucifer looks me directly in the eyes, staring into me as if he can *see* inside me. "Not tonight."

"But... but..." Marshall starts to sputter.

Lucifer's face hardens, his features as cold and harsh as the blizzard swirling in his irises. "Simon, remove him."

"No. No! I'll go!" Marshall says, panicked, and though I can't see what's going on due to the huge body blocking my view, I can hear a great deal of shuffling going on behind Lucifer.

Marshall grunts loudly and then there's a thump. "Hey! I'm going, I'm going!"

The bedroom door opens and then slams shut.

I jerk in Lucifer's arms in surprise but then feel all the fight go out of me. No matter how much I squirm, no matter how much I try to free myself from his grasp, I can't escape him. If anything, I feel like all my struggles have only tightened the grip he has on me.

Head dropping forward, I quiet my panting so I can

listen to Marshall stomping and continue to throw a tantrum about being removed from his own home.

After a minute, Lucifer sighs and I feel his grip loosen a little. "James, assist Simon. If Marshall wakes the children, feel free to make him regret it."

"Yes, boss," the second shadow answers and I don't even hear him as he walks out. I only know he's gone by the sound of the closing door.

A moment later there's some muffled arguing coming from the hallway then all goes quiet.

The seconds tick by. My panting slows as I catch my breath.

All at once I am suddenly aware that I'm alone with this strange man.

The air thickens.

Slowly, I lift my head and peer up at him. He's looking down at me so intensely I gasp.

My gasp seems to amuse him, and a slow smile spreads across his lips.

I stare at him in disbelief, my mind racing a mile a minute, trying to process everything that just happened. My mouth feels dry and my stomach is twisted. I want to believe this is a nightmare, that I'm still sleeping in my bed.

My husband didn't just trade me and our children away to save his own neck. He couldn't... He wouldn't...

Yet the fingers tightening around my arms remind me that he did.

I can't let this happen. I can't accept this. I have to

protect my children. He cannot have them! I won't let him hurt them.

Gathering up every ounce of courage I have inside me, I lift my chin and say, "You can't have us. We're not objects you can own or trade away at whim. I am a *person*, a person with rights, and I will not stand for this!"

Lucifer's eyes twinkle at me and it's so condescending I just want to spit in his face.

My anger only seems to amuse him even more. Head tipping back, he chuckles with mirth and just as I start to struggle again, he lifts me up.

It only takes him two long strides and then he throws me.

I go flying through the air and land on my bed with a grunt.

He's not far behind me, and quickly I get to my hands and knees, scooting back as he approaches.

Long, strong fingers going to the bottom of his suit jacket, he begins to unbutton it as he asks me, "Who's going to stop me?"

NEWSLETTER

Sign up for our newsletter - no spam- and download an
Izzy Sweet book for **free**

Dirty Nothings
PUBLISHING

http://bookhip.com/CKHPSJ

Made in United States
Troutdale, OR
02/19/2024

17798056R00181